Bruce Corbett's Speculative Short Stories

A collection of short stories

(This collection includes several short stories that were previously released individually.)

by Bruce Corbett

ISBN: 978-1-7380048-6-7

FOREWORD

I have to admit it. Writing short stories is hard! Each of the following stories have been re-written anywhere up to a hundred times. The stories I managed to place in magazines were ruthlessly stripped of any and all excess verbiage - a painful process for one who is in love with words. Novels allow a little meandering. Short stories do not.

The first of these stories first saw light when I was a university student. It is fun, when I put them together for this book, to re-read them and see the evolution of my thinking. The truth is, they were written over a forty year span. I hope you enjoy reading them as much as I did writing them.

The author

Bruce Corbett

TABLE OF CONTENTS

I had just read somewhere that the United States had more gun stores than gas stations. Students had been shot at Columbine, and the National Rifle association had reportedly offered each teacher in the country a free hand gun. The absurdities of these items led me to sit down and write an extrapolation. What would happen in staid Toronto if Quebec separated and Ontario joined the United States? Here is a fantasy - or is it? As I write this introduction, gang members in Toronto are well-armed and are currently shooting each other, while a U.S. lawyer is suing a dry cleaner who supposedly lost his favorite pair of pants for 65 million dollars. This story first appeared in the Fall 1999 edition of PERIDOT.

1. SHOPPING

"HONNNNEY."

Damn it! I knew that tone. It was no siren call, to lure me on to the rocks of connubial bliss. I wish! It was the call of the dreaded Mildred. I sighed and answered. Our house wasn't so large that I could hide or anything. "I'm in the bathroom, dear."

"Honey! Just as soon as you're done in there, I want you to pick up a few things for me at Loblaw's."

I thought through the implications of that apparently simple request and groaned. It was my birthday, after all. Wasn't there some law that says that you can stay home and relax on your own birthday? And what she was asking was nothing less than death defying.

Ever since the last Mr. Donut closed, even the police didn't go out on the streets at night. I can't say I blamed them. Ever since Quebec separated and Ontario became the fifty-third state, the guns had flowed north. Not Saturday night specials. Not semi-automatic military knock offs. No way. The real thing; fully automatic assault weapons; Uzis, MAC's, machine guns.

For a while Ontario was the third largest importer of weapons in the world. Boring Ontario changed. I sighed again. I knew SHE didn't really care what I thought about it. We both knew that I was on my way just as soon as I abandoned the shelter of the bathroom.

"It's pretty late, dear! It could be dangerous."

"Oh don't be silly, honey. Take the Humvee. I went by the armorers just yesterday. I had the oil checked and the gas tank filled. The ammo pods are all topped up, and they had a special on Big Berthas, so I told him to install one. You'll be as safe as if you are in your own snug little bed."

I wondered about that. The crime rate had climbed another 232% in the last year, but on the other hand, my bed shared by a cranky Mildred, was not the most secure place in the world, either.

I could only sit on the throne for so long. Eventually my bottom became so numb that I had to get up. I had already finished all the good literature I had stashed under the sink. I dutifully ran the water so I wouldn't get another lecture on personal cleanliness, and then headed out for the necessary briefing. My darling wife tucked the grocery list into my shirt pocket, and then sent me off with a supercilious peck on my cheek. I was heading down the basement steps when a deep growl told me that my BELOVED had decided to get another replacement Doberman. The last one had succumbed to a love tap from my gentle wife.

By the tone of its growl, it wasn't about to let me pass unchallenged. I waved my left hand in front of me as a tempting doggy snack as I used my right to grab for the Taser in my belt. The ten thousand volts gave the stupid animal temporary electronic rigor mortis, and I made it unscathed to the garage. Maybe it would remember to leave me alone the next time I had to pass through the nether regions of my own home.

I shrugged on my new flak jacket. It was a deep forest green, and had been my big present for my birthday. Mildred had hunted far and wide for one with such casual lines, yet one that could hide a brace of MAC 12's without a single telltale bulge or trace. Making sure that both hidden pockets had their complement of MAC's, I slipped behind the wheel of the massive armored beast that lurked in our garage. Then I flipped on the onboard AI I had nicknamed Ricky, after a character from an ancient madcap vid my granddad used to drag out for me whenever I became too obstreperous for his taste. As long as I was within a block of the house, Ricky plugged into the home security system by remote. The house AI was a little flaky, so I had named it Lucy, after the nutcase in the same series.

"Ricky, plug me direct into Lucy. Lucy, scan outside the door for life signs."

The deep tones of Ricky's synthesized masculine voice was replaced with the more dulcet tones of the Gerrald 4200 home security 'puter. The new tone was incongruous, coming from a couple of tons of macho machine. "Done, master."

"And?"

"And I am done, master."

'Puters can sure do some neat things, but they aren't as bright as the average three year old. "And are there any life signs within a range of 100 meters around the garage door?"

"No, master."

I had a sudden flashback from the days of my childhood, where I just used to open the door, after putting on my flack jacket, and headed out to play, safe and secure in the confines of our own unfenced property. The world had been so much safer then, and innocent. When had it all changed? I sighed. I had a job to do. I just didn't want to do it. "And how about around the side gate?"

"No one, master . . . Hold for further update."

I suddenly heard the hollow clattering of a 9 mm roof turret gun. "Lucy, I thought that you said there was no sign of any life form nearby!"

"There was briefly a life sign at the walkway gate. It carried pizza, but it did not know the password of the day, nor did it bother to identify itself as it stepped onto the property."

"You said 'briefly'."

"The life form entered the kill zone without permission, master."

The evening suddenly seemed much hotter. I pulled at my open collar, and started to work on my rapidly escalating breathing. Shit! The police would be pissed. That was the second time my wife had ordered pizza without bothering to tell the store all the details of our new security system. I just prayed that the guy was well onto our property before Lucy cut loose. Our insurance had doubled after the last incident.

"O.K., Lucy. Open both the garage door and the driveway gate on my command, and sterilize the garage after I leave . . . Now!"

I waited until the garage door was high enough that

the big buggy could slip under it, and then gunned it. The electrified gates swivelled open at my approach, and in the rearview mirror I saw the garage door descending. I didn't worry much about the 17 seconds that the garage was vulnerable. I knew that Lucy would flood the interior with an obnoxious gas, and then pump it out so it would be safe for my return. I had programmed Lucy to back up the gassing with the basement-level mobile defensive mini-pod, and the walking appetite was loose somewhere in the lower level, or would be if it had stopped twitching. Anyway, I figured that anyone who made it into the house through all that had to be pretty talented.

I hit the road at a respectable fifty kilometers an hour, and the big machine drifted right. Damn! Almost immediately I hit a couple of 2x4 strips studded with nasty spikes. I thanked God that the last time I had the Beast in for a retread, I had sprung for the puncture-proof Goodyears. I slipped over the vicious spikes with hardly a hiss of escaping air; but lots of screams of rage from the Street Rovers who hovered nearby and had hoped for someone helpless to beat on. I knew that Ricky had been programmed by my bloodthirsty wife to respond to any such perceived threat with a stream of 9 mm lead. I was sure that I didn't have sufficient 'clear intent' on these guys' part to litter the road with corpses, so I hurriedly called out to the AI.

"Ricky, no one is to get shot! Swivel the turret to five o'clock and put a three second burst over their heads." As it was, the chatter of the small caliber slugs just made the punks jump for shelter. The staccato sounds almost matched the thundering of my heart. I practiced more deep breathing as I rounded the corner on to Royal York and punched the accelerator. It didn't do any good. What I mean to say is, the accelerator worked OK, but my pulse rate was surpassing my best bowling score. Hell, I didn't want to shoot anybody. I just wanted to go to the damned grocery store!

I drifted left onto Bloor, and I felt a little more secure on the main drag. There were no obvious danger points, and, after dark, I simply didn't stop at red lights.

I cruised the couple of miles to my wife's favorite Loblaw's, and then slowed down to check out the parking lot. Damn! The road itself was clear enough, but a trio of old junkers had been parked across the entrance to the supermarket. I could call the police, but they would only arrive with the sun. Or I could cruise around waiting for the bad guys to leave, or I ran out of gas. At night, in suburban Toronto, the gas trick wasn't a bright thing to do. I outweighed each of the cars by a factor of three to one, I was armored, and my wife's instructions were crystal clear. The idea of facing a dozen armed strangers was less terrifying to me than the thought of facing my spouse with empty hands, so I decided that I couldn't back down. I decided to go for a parking spot!

I aimed the beast, worked on squeezing my bladder muscles a little tighter, and headed for the totally inadequate opening. I heard Ricky cocking something a lot bigger than the twin 9 mm's mounted on the roof, and suddenly remembered that my wife had ordered a monster 50-caliber machine gun to be installed.

I was terrified that Ricky would do something precipitate. Until someone provided me indisputable evidence of the infamous 'clear intent', I could not let Ricky activate the big gun. The insurance companies got really cranky if you took precipitate action without some pretty good evidence . . . and I was born Canadian, for heaven's sake! I don't even like guns! We former Canadians had finally bought the line that if everybody was armed, then the bad guys left you alone.

What really happened was that the bad guys just went out and bought a bigger weapon than you had. And they were ready to use theirs. So far these particular hoods had done nothing worse than litter the parking lot with their junky cars and themselves. The guys did seem pissed that I didn't have any inclination to stop and pay a toll or get mugged. As I kept the big machine grinding towards them, they began to wave assorted assault weapons in my direction. I ordered Ricky to fisheye the video-cam. I wasn't making a Hollywood movie, but I sure as hell would need something for the insurance company vultures if Ricky cut loose with Big Bertha and somebody got hurt.

My dilemma was solved. One tattooed thug, tall and cadaverous in the artificial light, got mad enough at me that he leveled his AK 74 and let fly. My behemoth was armored, and his bullets were no more annoying than whining mosquitoes, but it was the excuse Ricky was programmed to wait for.

I yelled desperately. "Ricky, shoot at the middle car; not the man!"

I almost peed when Ricky fired a five second burst in the car's general direction. I was awed. My big machine was slowed by the savage kick of the bullets, and the punk's car just flew apart. The guy looked as startled as I was, and it was rather comical how he did a backwards flip to get away from the lead and the tons of steel and Kevlar that was coming at him.

As the Humvee crunched through the very-recently vacated area between the two remaining illegally parked heaps, Ricky popped the tear-gas canisters on either side of the Humvee. For good measure, the AI then popped two smoke canisters.

The punks wouldn't be able to see me for awhile, and I knew that my Mildred had been naughty. She had told Horst Schniber, our personal armorer, to add a little something special to the regulation-issue tear gas. It wouldn't kill the punks, but it would sure help them clean out their systems; from both ends. Horst had assured

Mildred that it would disperse quickly and leave few residual traces in the bloodstream for eager-beaver lawyer types to get hyped over.

I slammed the big machine into a skid barely thirty feet from the main entrance. I knew that I was parked illegally, but damn it, it was night time, no police were going to be driving by for quite some time, and I was plain terrified of being out in the open at all.

Unclipping the velcro patches and freeing up my personal armament, I raced for the door. I had to let go of one of the MACs to open the door. I wondered why they always opened automatically as you left, but you had to open the damned things manually when you arrived. What if I had to carry stuff in? What if I didn't buy anything? What if my life was endangered because I had to stand there while I tugged the f#*king doors open?

The distance was short, however, and even with the brief pause I had to make to wrestle the doors open, I was safely inside within seconds. I walked gingerly towards the greeter in the Plexiglas machine-gun nest, and slowly and ostentatiously checked my two MAC 12s.

The big-bore gun followed me every step of the way. I didn't really mind. After a couple of hundred robberies, the store had finally got some decent security. Anybody who argues with a 50-caliber is stupid! I knew. I had just seen one - mine - in operation.

I made it through the metal and nitrogen sniffers, and a shopping-cart rolled over to greet me. The stupid piece of silicon-on-wheels insisted on squawking about all the specials I was passing by as I prowled the aisles with my wife's list clutched in my sweaty hand. Finally I stuffed a credit card inside its maw, and it condescended to follow silently.

After almost twenty minutes of cruising the aisles, I had everything Mildred had asked for. I acquiesced to the rape of my bank account by the checkout 'puter, and then

I headed for the main door. Slipping my twin MAC's back into their pouches, I felt the barrel of the 50-caliber tracking me again. After watching what mine had done outside, I was not about to tempt fate by annoying the pretty little pony-tailed blond who handled it.

Slowly, I reached into my pants pocket and extracted the key fob. I pushed the first button, and the behemoth just outside rumbled into life. Now came the dangerous part. I stepped forward so the door sensor would know I wanted to exit, and, as soon as the opening was large enough for me to squeeze through, I ran through the door and simultaneously pushed the second button.

The Humvee's security system was now down, and that made me really nervous. There were a bunch of guys out there who would likely be pretty cranked with me, if they were through puking and changing their pants. I compensated for my fear by pulling one of the MACs free while I tried to hang on to the bag of groceries with my other arm.

I started to sprint the thirty feet to the vehicle. Almost before I cleared the supermarket door, a gaunt and unshaven bum materialized in front of me. He could have been just trying to steal the Humvee, but I don't think so. Anyone who was unable to sweet-talk Ricky would have found the cabin filled with a particularly nasty gas ten seconds after the machine started rolling. That particular system had been standard in Humvee-General Ford Motors vehicles for several years, and even an ignorant bum would know that. That left me as the prime target. He didn't leave me guessing long.

"Mister, hand over all your money! Do it quick, now!"

I wondered what asshole would try and ask for cash in this day and age! You have to be pretty stupid to make a living stealing cash. Nobody bothered carrying any. Actually, he did look stupid, but the Barretta he was waving was real. I just hoped that the Humvee security camera was still on. Figuring I had sufficient evidence of 'clear intent' even for a petty insurance adjustor, I squeezed both my sphincter muscles and my eyes real tight, and pressed the trigger of the MAC. It was partly hidden behind the grocery bag, and I hoped that SHE WHO HAD SENT ME would forgive a few holes in the bread.

The man, obviously too stupid or too poor to buy a decent bullet-proof jacket, pitched forward. I shoved the groceries into my vehicle, followed quickly by a flustered owner who needed to change his pants as soon as possible. From inside the car I practiced my projectile vomiting. As a soft ex-Canadian, I just wasn't used to blowing people away.

What a day! In one hour, I had just blown up a car and blown away a stranger. My house had massacred a pizza delivery boy, and my wife's damned guard Doberman had tried to have me for his late night snack. My insurance rates were no doubt on their way up again, and, truth to tell, that last guy would have got me had he been just a little brighter or a little quicker. Only sheer terror had caused me to pull that trigger.

I hoped that the ride home would be uneventful, but I guess I should have known better. There were few vehicles out there, 'cept maybe a loaded semi, that could stop a stubborn Humvee.

At night time, drivers generally stayed far away from each other. More and more vehicles had weapons pods, an American fashion innovation that had quite quickly migrated to America's newest state. They were generally a good hint that someone was prepared to defend their own.

I knew that the Humvee was almost invulnerable from casual interference, but just the week before I had downloaded web reports of a terrifying new tactic. While a driver was distracted, a second vehicle slapped a claymore on the armored vehicle. After that, you got to negotiate; very carefully. One wrong move, and both you and your mighty vehicle are toast.

Thus, when I saw a junker catching up with me, I felt the familiar hordes of butterflies starting their regular migration around my very empty and unhappy stomach. I was momentarily tempted to drop an oil slick and pop the caltrops, but the potential litigation costs for accidental collateral damage were astronomical. I was haunted by the 'clear intent' clause so beloved of the ambulance-chasing shysters.

I couldn't outrun the car, so I ordered Ricky to activate the weapons systems. I had no intention of using the nasty stuff, but I hoped that the sight of Big Bertha and the twin 9 mm's rotating towards them might make them a little anxious. It sure scared the hell out of me!

The car pulled parallel with me, and I must admit, I suddenly forgot to watch the rearview mirror. A girl in the back seat stuck her body part-way out of the window and waved gaily to me. It was hard not to be distracted. The girl was cute, and as naked as the day she was born. I couldn't help but admire her various assets. It had been a long time since Mildred had looked like that. Come to think of it, Mildred had never looked like that.

The distinctive click of a claymore mine magnetically attaching on the back of the Humvee brought me back to reality in a great hurry. A second car, driving without lights and armed with a telescopic lance with a mine perched on the end of it, had unobtrusively maneuvered into place behind me. His job done, the driver quickly dropped back. Horst had told Mildred about the new trick, and for once, SHE WHO NEVER LISTENED had.

"Ricky, blow the metal panel covering the rear of the Humvee!"

"Yes, sahib!"

I briefly wondered just what kind of programming my wife was giving the AI, but a muffled explosion brought me back to the present in a great hurry, and verified that Ricky had followed my instructions. The claymore, fastened by strong magnetic clamps, stayed with the sheet of ferrous metal, which now savagely attacked the car following behind.

The girl was either counting to one or giving me the finger, but I just smiled and enjoyed watching her boobs bouncing up and down. Mildred no longer wanted to share her mammary glands with me. In their present condition, I wasn't sure I really cared. Ricky continued to aim the 9 mm turret in the general direction of the second car, but that car peeled away.

The rest of the ride home was uneventful. The Street Rovers had even removed their tire puncture strips from the road in front of my house. Perhaps the business end of my turret had persuaded them that they would have better luck elsewhere. More likely they were happily raping someone on the next block.

"Ricky. Tell Lucy to open the main gate, starting . . . now!"

I sailed through the gates and headed directly for the garage. Lucy's rear roof turret covered my approach, and I slipped into the garage safe and sound.

After parking the Big Beast, I took a few moments to recover. I was drenched in sweat and breathing hard from the stress of the trip. My stomach was one tight knot. I felt like a human doormat. For years I had paid the bills, and did what I was told. Righteous anger flowed through me. Just for once I was going to stand up to the DRAGON LADY. When I didn't want to go out; I wouldn't! Steeling myself to face what was waiting for me upstairs, I picked up the grocery bag and called out my challenge. "Honey, I'm home!"

Mildred stood waiting for me by the refrigerator. She looked cranky, a sure sign of pizza deprivation. She graciously hammer-locked the grocery bag and proceeded to wrestle it the last three meters to the counter, where she dumped its precious cargo on to the counter. She turned angrily to me.

"There are bullet holes in my special bread . . . And I told you to get the one percent milk! You know I'm on a diet . . . You're just going to have to go right back down there and get the proper milk, like I told you to do!"

When the police arrived the next morning, I was at a loss to explain how an intruder had got through our sophisticated defense system. It was incredibly sad. Using one of my very own MAC's, some sadist had held down the trigger until my mate had been virtually cut in two by the vicious stream of bullets. Aroused from my sleep by the ripping thunder of bullets, I had rushed downstairs with the other MAC, which I had taken up to the bedroom to clean. I had sprayed in the direction of the departing figure, but in my terror, I had apparently not hit the person. The intruder had got away, along with the whole box that contained Lucy's CPU and her stored memory crystals, as well as a fair hunk of my wife's jewelry.

I was devastated, and the police were most solicitous. I told them about the thugs who had tried to rob me at Loblaw's, and the police speculated that one of them might have been able to follow me home. The police Lieutenant offered to take me to a protected compound for a few days, but I demurred. I told them I just wanted to be alone with my grief. I watched the armored police chopper lift off, and then headed back inside. Next I had a Doberman to gas.

The second millennium was quickly coming to an end and the pressures from an overwhelming counseling workload were building. There was only one rational solution. I escaped into a world of fantasy every chance I got. Instead of runaways and would-be suicides, I faced evil emperors and some of the most deadly dinosaurs that ever lived. In Man's First Enemy, I wrote of encounters between man and dinosaurs from the dinosaurs' point of view. In the interest of fairness, here is the other side of the story.

2. THE HUNTERS

The air shimmered strangely, and then there was a rush of displaced molecules. Suddenly a huge globular contrivance materialized in the Cretaceous meadow. The ferns and primitive trees were crushed by the massive weight.

A portal irised, and five human shapes stepped down onto ground that had disappeared under a kilometer of water before, paradoxically, their first ancestors had stood upright. Three were dressed in the best tradition of African safaris, and the remaining two were dressed in blue working denim. All carried Kalashnikov AK 94s, but the two in denim also had an assortment of other objects strapped to their backs.

Safari Suit One, Lord Eaton-Jones by name, was tall, thin, and the haughty end-product of generations of selective British inbreeding. The lord carefully clicked off the safety of his weapon, and turned to Little Pete, the assistant guide.

"I say. Just why did you give us these rifles?"

"Mister, when you're 70 million years from home and you could be facing hundreds of tons of charging meat and teeth, you want a gun with a lot of stopping power, and one that won't jam up, no matter what. The army M23s, now, are nice guns, built to fine tolerances, but these babies were built to be dependable in Russian mud and winter. If they'll work there, they'll work anywhere, anytime. They may not be quite so accurate on single fire, but you just hold the trigger down for a while and watch what happens. Get a little dirt in it, and it just keeps on punching lead."

Jeff Killroy, the third client in the exclusive safari, was American. The portly multi-billionaire was considerably older than his two comrades, and bald. He held the weapon awkwardly, and spoke in a deep and resonant voice.

"Just how do we get away with using these things, anyway? I thought that it was TimeTrav's cardinal rule that we don't disturb the local fauna."

Big John, the professional guide and leader of the safari, responded. "Mr. Killroy, the rules say that you can use weapons only in self defense. Trust me, you see a Tyrannosaurus in full charge, you're going to feel a sudden need to defend yourself. These animals are for real. They will eat you if they can catch you. They ain't got large brains, but their stomachs are generally empty, and their teeth are almighty big!"

Even as they spoke, a herd of mixed herbivores drifted gradually back into sight. Their primitive brains now accepted that the stationary globe was in no way making hostile moves toward them, and the five small creatures beside it were too far away and too puny to be worth any serious consideration.

The five stood idly watching the herd and admiring the sun-swept savannah, interspersed occasionally with copses of primitive trees and modern oaks and hickories. Finally, when the tourists had rubbernecked long enough, the two guides unloaded the two Hover-Jeeps, and, after turning on a force field that was capable of keeping their time machine safe even from a cranky Tyrannosaurus Rex, they loaded up the three safari suits and set off on their Cretaceous adventure.

Lucy Bauer, the lone female in the group, spoke up for the very first time when the guides stopped the vehicles at the top of a rise overlooking the otherwise flat savannah. The woman was only in her late twenties, and very shy, though obviously rich enough to pay for the incredibly expensive journey through time.

"Have any humans ever visited this exact time era before?"

Big John was a powerful looking man. He hooked his thumbs in his belt, looked deliberately at the rich client, and let his gaze run insolently from head to toes. Only when he finished his survey did he answer.

"Not exactly, Miss. Paleontologists and Biologists have made repeated trips to this era, but you're talking millions of years, and, anyways, the laws of Temporal Displacement don't allow anyone to come twice to within a hundred years of this specific time frame. Even that is considered a close call, and, to be safe, the regs say no second group can come within a thousand years. They hope, that way, to ensure that there is no possible permanent temporal disturbance caused by our visits."

"But then how do you know it's safe for us to be here?"

"Now, Miss. The scientists have bracketed the era by

a million years on either side. And we've been on several safaris within this time frame, give or take a couple of million years. We have the best protective equipment available, and the force fields are invulnerable. You don't have to worry your pretty little head about a thing!"

Even as he spoke, a giant Alamosaurus lumbered from the swamp just visible to their left. The huge creature towered over the herd of mixed Triceratops, Duckbills, and Anklyosaurs, who were themselves giant by the standards of the human era. As the gigantic animal plodded toward a copse of trees, the very ground shook. The herbivores instinctively knew that this slow-moving giant was not a threat, but still sidled out of its direct path.

Lucy grew excited. "Wow! That must be one of the biggest things that ever lived on the face of the earth! Can we get closer? I want to take some pictures!"

Big John, the leader, responded. "Yes, ma'am, we'll tour around the herds tomorrow. But you will have to stay in the vehicle, and we can't get too close to the animals. The Triceratops down there - the ones with three horns on their heads? They ain't too bright, but if they decide that you're a danger, they form a defensive ring, and several of the old bulls are likely to charge out at us. They can run faster than you think, and the Hover-Jeeps are little protection if they catch up to us."

Lucy spoke in a squeaky voice that reflected her anxiety. "Then how do we protect ourselves from them?"

"Simple, Miss. We don't bother them, and they don't bother us. They're not the ones you have to worry about, anyway."

"So what do we do?"

"That's easy. We set up a force-field perimeter where we camp, just like we left around the time capsule, and,' he smiled, 'I always have ol' Betsy."

With that he dexterously unslung the tube that he had been carrying on his back, and unclipped it.

Jeff Killroy reacted. 'Holy shit! That's a LAW-2! Surely TimeTrav doesn't allow those things back in time?!"

Big John continued. "Well, we didn't actually ask anyone, but if you see tons of hungry animal coming at you, you'll be glad we brought ol' Betsy along. With a full anti-matter load, this baby will not only stop a Tyrannosaurus cold; it'll make it bloody disappear."

Little Pete horned in. "Bloody is the right word. It rains T-Rex! But remember, if you don't totally stop a Rex, it'll just keep on coming. They ain't got enough brains to stop once they decide that you're dinner."

Even as they spoke, there was a stirring in the herd. A cacophony of bellows and grunts indicated an increasing anxiety, then suddenly the Duckbills were bugling in alarm. The entire mixed herd started to surge toward the east, leaving the Alamosaurus standing alone.

Big John turned quickly to Little Pete. "Damn! Something bad is coming our way! Get the force-field generators in place, now!"

While the three tourists watched in alarm, the two guides leapt from the vehicles and feverishly set up the four force-field generators in a square around the little party.

Big John yelled at the bald American. "You! Killroy! Get that fuel cell on the ground and get the cables over here, fast!"

Jeff Killroy, majority shareholder of over three dozen separate major corporations, looked indignant. "I thought you just said that your toy would vaporize a full-sized charging Tyrannosaurus."

"It will, Mister, but there's worse things than a T-Rex on these plains. Get those damn wires over here now!"

Lord Robert Eaton-Jones had been listening attentively. He quickly wiped the sweat from his brow, grabbed the wires, and ran them across to Big John. As he handed the man the power wires, he asked the question that had been praying on his mind.

"I say, old boy! Just what is more dangerous than one of the largest carnivores that ever lived?"

"That's easy, Sir Robert. T-Rex is big but stupid, and there ain't so many of them. How'd you like to meet about twenty junior-size T-Rexes, with the brains to hunt as a team? Name's Dromaeosaurus. They ain't so big and strong as the T-Rex, but they think, and there's a whole lot of them coming at you at once. They can absorb a lot of bullets before they go down, and they're smart enough to set up an ambush. Even the LAW-2 can't take them all out at once. Until we know exactly what's happening out there, it's just safer to get the force-fence in place and activated."

A slight hum and the tiniest ripple in the air indicated that an encircling force field had cut in. Big John finished adjusting the generator, and then turned back with a smile on his face.

"O.K., folks. You can relax and wander around, but don't walk into the force field. You can exit through it O.K., but an A-bomb won't get you back inside the perimeter unless one of us sees you're outside and turns the field off. I've adjusted it so nothing larger than a rabbit can come this way. That way you feel the breeze and get fresh air, but nothing nasty can get to us. The only things that can get to us are insects, and you'll be thrilled to know that the mosquitoes back here haven't figured out how to bite yet. So relax and enjoy the view. We should soon see what the fuss out there is all about."

His words were prophetic, for as he spoke, a pack of some twenty man-sized and two-legged dinosaurs tore into sight. Tails straight behind them, they ran at the speed of a racehorse.

Fanning out, several of them tried to turn the last remaining herd beasts toward their comrades, but the herds had had too much warning, and all were moving at high speed directly away from the carnivore pack. Only the Alamosaurus was left. The savage hunters swerved, and quickly circled the huge beast. The tiny head on the enormous neck swung comically from side to side in a vain attempt to keep the fast-moving hunters in sight.

Lucy Bauer spoke up. "My God! They really are hunting in tandem! Can they really pull down such a giant?"

Big John responded. "I don't think so, Miss. Its skin would be a challenge even for those guys, and the Alamosaurus isn't as helpless as it looks. They've been known to crush a T-Rex."

Jeff Killroy looked indignant. "How could even one of those things kill a T-Rex?"

"Easy, mister. It rears up on those hind legs, and then it falls on the Rex. Nothing survives under one of those babes!"

Both tourists and guides watched the encounter in fascination. The carnivores started to dart in and slash at the legs that were like giant tree-trunks. The giant reacted. A sweep of its huge tail caught three of the agile hunters, and they were thrown over fifty feet through the air. Only one was able to regain its feet.

Big John giggled loudly. "Hey, partner. Let's give 'em a little hand. Give me a HE load."

The head guide expertly clicked open the LAW-2 with a few deft twists, and Little Pete clipped a bright red head on to the rocket before the safari suits even knew what was happening. The thin red beam of the laser sight lanced out at the giant dinosaur, followed a second later by the flaring rocket. Even at a subsonic speed, the rocket impacted within seconds. The Alamosaurus had its lower guts blown open. The body swayed several times, and then toppled ponderously onto its side as the neural messages finally made it to the tiny brain. The

Dromaeosaurs were startled by the thunderous explosion, and quickly retreated a few hundred feet. The huge pile of meat was an irresistible magnet, however, and over the next few minutes they circled warily closer.

Little Pete started giggling again. "Dinner's served, boys. Compliments of TimeTrav. Tell all your friends about our friendly service!"

The fierce carnivores continued circling, though the ring tightened. At last the largest dashed in, while the others paused and watched. Assured that there was no further danger, the leader threw himself on the huge pile of meat. The rest of the pack then closed with a rush. Sections of the giant's back were heavily armored, and even the Dromaeosaurs' powerful jaws and sharp teeth were unable to tear through the skin there, but the soft underbelly had been torn apart by the rocket charge, and the animals congregated there.

Little Pete turned to the three shocked tourists. "Now you just watch those bastards! They're as well organized as a wolf pack. Don't tell me they don't have brains!"

Lucy had jumped from her seat when the rocket was fired. She waved her arms and squeaked in indignation. "You shot that beautiful beast! It was no threat to us! How could you do such a thing!?"

Big John just smiled as he watched the feeding frenzy at the base of the hill. "Look, Missy, we promised to show you the animal life here. With a bit of luck, that pile of meat down there will attract the T-Rex hisself. You ain't seen nothing until you've seen one of the Big Guys!"

Lord Eaton Jones suddenly pointed to the sky. "I say, look at that!"

Little Pete squinted and put his hand to his forehead to act as a shade. "That there is a Quetzalcoatlus. It's the biggest damn thing that ever flew. Those wings stretch over 50 feet across. The bastard's just riding the thermals.

It'll wait to see what will be left over, unless it gets hungry enough or stupid enough to take on a Dromaeosaur pack. They don't generally try that but once!"

Trapped within the narrow confines of the force field, the safari members made the most of the situation and set up camp where they were. The two guides set up four sleeping tents, a second toilet shelter for the benefit of Lucy, and then set to rustling up some dinner.

The Safari Suits continued to watch in awe as the carnivores ate themselves into a stupor, and the sky gradually filled with giant flying dinosaurs. Beyond the site of the kill, the plains gradually filled again with the grazers, though none came close, and all kept a wary eye on the Dromaeosaur pack.

Shortly before sunset, the Duckbills began their bugling again. Several of the ungainly creatures reared up to extend their range of vision. Even the feeding carnivores showed nervousness, sniffing the air and standing upright. Two scouts finally left the pack and started coursing to the west.

The puzzle was settled in minutes, however. A deep roar reverberated across the savannah, and the Anklyosaurs and Duckbills again broke into wild flight. The Triceratops flowed smoothly into a tight ring, with the youngsters on the inside. An impenetrable wall of horns and bone faced outward.

A great bronze beast ran into sight. It towered some twenty feet into the air, and ran on two powerful legs. As fast and powerful looking as it was however, what was most noticeable was its oversized head and its rows of dagger-like teeth. All three Safari Suits knew without asking that the king of the carnivores, the Tyrannosaurus Rex, had arrived on the scene.

The two Dromaeosaur scouts returned to the pack at a full run, and they all, grumbling and growling, started to move away from the giant carcass. They did not panic, but alertly stayed out of reach of their giant cousin. The Tyrannosaurus, for its part, was not interested in any of the very agitated and alert herd animals. It headed directly toward the dead Alamosaurus. The beast passed near the Triceratops ring, and, to the surprise of the tourists, two massive bulls charged out from the ring and ran directly at the Tyrannosaurus. Their speed was phenomenal, but the Tyrannosaurus simply picked up its own speed, and the bulls stopped once they considered the carnivore to be safely away from the herd.

The three tourists watched in awe as the huge predator tore into the dead dinosaur. Unlike his smaller cousins, it was quite capable of rending the thickest skin. The Quetzalcoatluses circling overhead screamed in frustration, but continued in their aerial loops. They knew that even the mighty Tyrannosaurus could not eat all of the mountain of meat that lay at its feet. They were just impatient for their turn to come.

The pack of Dromaeosaurs, already sated, abandoned their claim and trotted off to the west. The professional guides served their clients barbecued steak and potatoes from seventy million years in the future, while the threesome sat fascinated, inhaling the sweet odors of flowering plants and watching the pre-historic drama that continued to enfold right in front of their eyes.

At last the sun set, and darkness hid the events on the plain from view. The campfire gradually burned itself out, and the three tourists retired to their tents for some sleep. The guides sat around the dying embers of the fire. Little Pete spoke to his senior partner.

"So, do we take turns on sentry duty?"

"Nah. What for? No dinosaur's going to get through the force field. If it will make you feel better, though, you can hook one of the Jeep's power supplies onto the fuel cell. That way the field will have lots of reserve power if something does try to take it on. After you do that, feel free to turn in."

"Okay, boss."

The little creature waited until even the dim light of the moon faded. In a world of huge and powerful predators, small mammals had to be furtive and alert. It had an advantage over the small dinosaurs and reptiles of its age, however. Since it was able to regulate its own body temperature, it was capable of quick movement even in the cold of the night. It was a slim advantage, but it gave it some hope of survival in a world of exothermic animals.

There was a major penalty for the advantage of night-time mobility, however. The small furry creature was required to eat almost ten times as much food per pound of body weight as its cold-blooded rivals. Thus it scuttled about, desperately hungry, in the night. It was irresistibly drawn by the tantalizing odors of food.

There were strange shapes on the hilltop, but the strong aroma of meat drew it forward in spite of its instincts. As it approached the mysterious site, it felt its body hit an invisible barrier. Fear flooded its senses, but the odor of food was still strong. When no further discomfort ensued, it moved slightly to the right and tried to advance again.

This time the animal, no larger than a twentieth century squirrel, found that it could move forward, with only a slight tingling in its extremities. The animal's exquisitely sensitive sense of smell led it to a carelessly discarded bone, but there was little meat left on it, and the mammal didn't have the powerful teeth needed to reach the marrow. Still hungry, but extremely wary, it proceeded to explore the alien camp further.

As the small creature passed a box on the ground, it scented salt. Salt was a rare commodity on the savannah, and the animals were forced to get their body salts from what they ate. Excited by the heady smell of salt, its nose started twitching. The sensitive nostrils led it unerringly to two cables that had been handled by a sweaty British lord. The odor of the alien animal was frightening, but the salt was an irresistible temptation.

It attempted to strip the salt molecules from the wires. Its teeth, however, were very sharp, and the bite severed one of the twin wires. The electrons flowed from the wire, through the little mammal, and into the ground.

The powerful surge burned the animal's mouth, which sent the primitive mammal spinning backwards. With the power source cut, the invisible force field immediately collapsed. The little animal lay rigid for a few seconds, and then scrambled to its feet. Dazed but terrified, it fled the hilltop encampment and scuttled for its subterranean burrow. There it would hide until the dark returned. Day was when the light and the warmth would rouse the exothermic creatures that so dominated its universe.

The leader of the Dromaeosaurus pack had spotted the alien creatures even before the pack had attacked the giant Alamosaurus. After being driven from the carcass, she had led her followers in a circling movement around to a dense copse on the other side of the camp. The pack-members had been full, and lethargic, but they were willing, as they were insatiably curious.

Most of them dozed, while one or two sentries watched from hiding for most of the night. They watched the human camp by inclination, and for Tyrannosaurus Rex out of prudent good sense. The gentle dawn breezes brought them the delicious aroma of mammalian meat, and the leader decided that once their bodies warmed a little, they would charge the strange nests that held the puzzling creatures.

The pack leader waited for the morning sun to warm her body. She was anxious that the overgrown mammals would rouse the shiny flying-creatures that appeared to be willing to transport them, and perhaps defend them as well. The Hover-Jeeps remained parked, however, and the guides and their guests slept a good sleep.

The first warning came when a loud bellow was heard. All the humans woke with a start. The sound was enough to stampede herds on the savannah. Up close, it was a terrifying sound, and for the time-travelers, it was close!

Big John, well aware of the hunting cry of the Dromaeosaurs, roused enough to peek through his tent flap. He knew they were all safe behind the force field, but it sounded as if the savage hunters had decided to attack their encampment. He felt an instinctive dread of the ruthless hunters, and perhaps for that reason had in the past enjoyed picking them off when they had vainly thrown themselves at the protective force field. He was reaching for his Kalashnikov when a lumbering dinosaur body ran right past his tent! Realizing instantly that their protective shield was somehow down, he shook his partner awake, clipped on his gun belt, and grabbed his rifle.

Jeff Killroy was startled out of a deep sleep. He had been dreaming that he was young and handsome, as well as rich. The two beautiful girls faded as a deep bellow came from much too close. He sat up, naked, in his sleeping bag; puzzled and frightened. Two three-inch claws suddenly pierced the wall of his nylon tent, quickly followed by a larger shape that resolved itself into a massive head studded with fearsome teeth. The animal plainly did not know what to make of the tent material, but its novelty only delayed the creature for a few moments.

The fierce predator easily tore a hole large enough for its body to fit through. Jeff Killroy, scion of an old New England family, and holder of financial power that was greater than some entire countries, crawled to the rear of his tent and screamed. His rifle lay within reach, but it did not even occur to him to try and reach for it. His unexpected guest had no such pacific intention, however. It lurched into the tent through the now gaping hole, and seized the man's head in its mouth.

The thundering of feet told the newly roused humans that an entire pack of dinosaurs had somehow made it past the supposedly impenetrable force field. Lucy Bauer just stood and tried to cover her nudity as two monsters from her worst nightmare snuffled and slobbered in her tent, and then proceeded to eat her alive.

Lord Eaton Jones was a rich dilettante, but he had spent some years in his nation's navy, and was quite capable of protecting himself. When the wall of his tent dissolved into a hideous mouth studded with gaping teeth, he tried to reach for his assault rifle. He was a good marksman, having hunted trophy animals around the world. The gun had been stored right under where the first Dromaeosaur tore an opening, however, so he fought the attacking beasts with a short knife and his bare fists. He sliced one of the beasts twice before a razor talon tore into him.

The two guides were former marines, and were well trained in self-defense. It had been one of the prerequisites for employment with TimeTrav. Both were dressed within seconds, and they were prepared when their tent wall started tearing. Coolly and professionally, Big John fired short bursts from his Kalashnikov at the shadows that occasionally showed themselves as dinosaurs through the torn tent. He knew that most of their ammunition was stored in the Hover-Jeeps, and so he fired sparingly, in spite if the almost superstitious fear he felt for the Dromaeosaurs.

Some three monsters staggered back from his tent, each with serious wounds in its chest or head. In a killing frenzy driven by his fear, he took the attack to the enemy, stepping out through the new ragged doorway so recently torn in the side of his tent.

He dropped two more Dromaeosaurs before one managed to come at him from behind and knock the rifle from his grip. He turned to face the growling creature, filling his hands with his Ruger 9 mm pistol and Bowie knife. He stabbed at the leathery skin even while he fired point-blank into the eye sockets. He knew that many dinosaurs had very thick protective bones, and their brains were not large. He had been trained to go for the eye shot whenever possible.

The creature staggered back in shock from the twin blows, but still another Dromaeosaur caught at the guide from behind, and John felt the fetid breath of the carnivore while short but powerful arms pinioned him helplessly.

Little Pete, startled by a shape on the outside of the tent, emptied his clip in one continuous burst that tore one dinosaur in half, but left nothing to dissuade other attackers. He, too, managed to stab at one of the attackers as it tried to enter the tent, but another tore a second hole behind him, and the guide whirled too late. His single sharp blade wounded the dinosaur, but the huge mouth lunged for his head, and Little Pete barely felt the jaws snap shut.

The Dromaeosaurs abandoned the hilltop site once there was no meat left. They left the bodies of their egg-mates behind. They were instinctively reluctant to eat their own unless they were starving.

The sun rose steadily in the eastern sky, and the Hover-Jeeps sat patiently, waiting for their human passengers. It would be a thousand years before anyone would arrive to check on the safari party, but man would return. He would even take on the dinosaurs again, and, with a little help from a meteorite, he would manage to win.

In The Hunters several wealthy people traveled far into the past to observe the flora and fauna of the Cretaceous Age. A primitive mammal inadvertently shut down their security system, however, and the humans became food for a pack of intelligent dinosaurs. This story is the reciprocal. What would the story would be like from the other point of view? How would a dinosaur respond to humans and their machines? Here is my take on it. This short story was first published in SPACEWAY magazine in February of 2000.

3. MAN'S FIRST ENEMY

I led my egg-mates in the Direction-of-the-Setting-Sun. I was still in shock. Something huge and round had materialized near us even as we were resting under cover from our only enemy, Big-hunter. Twentieth-Born, the pack's youngest, wanted to investigate, but I growled caution. Something that large could be very dangerous. Smaller creatures had swarmed out of the globe, including two shiny-flying-creatures that floated on the air. The smaller animals looked like they could be edible, but there was no sense in attacking when the giant shining Egg/mother was so close. Thus we left the area of the mysterious giant Egg/mother, and I led the pack out on to the land-of-the-grass on a hunt. The herd of mixed Spiky-horns, Tall-standers and Spiny-backs were nearby, but even before we broke cover, part of the herd sensed our presence and started to grunt and bellow. The Tall-standers are the worst. When suspicious, they rise up as high on their hind legs as they can, and act as sentries. As soon as the first one spotted us, it started the damned bugling which is then echoed by all the rest of its kind. The result is instant stampede; away from us.

Third-Born and Fourth-Born tried arcing away from us in an attempt to herd some of the animals back our way, but the animals had got too great a head start. We had not eaten in several days, however, and hunger would soon make us weak. Having expended the energy we had to date, we went flat out. I signaled the pack to use their speed and we would see if there were any lame or injured animals which we could pull down. All twenty of us charged after the retreating herd at full speed. The land-of-the-grass cleared unfortunately quickly, but in the midst of the galloping animals stood a titan.

The Swamp-monster stared down benignly at us from his impressive height, but he did not hurry on his way. The giant monsters only feared my big cousin, the Big-hunter, and even then, in a one to one contest, it was not Big-hunter who always won. I would not have believed this myself, until I actually saw a Swamp-monster rear up, and simply fall on an attacking Big-hunter. NOTHING could survive having a full-grown Swamp-monster fall on it!

Well, our strategy had got us nothing but tired and more hungry. In sheer frustration, Nineteenth and Twentieth-Born attacked the Swamp-monster. It was rather comical, for they could only run around its legs as if they were circling giant tree trunks. They were the more recently hatched members of the pack, and they were still full of the ignorance of youth. Still, some of the other members of the pack joined in the game. I should have snorted a retreat, but I was too slow.

Several of the youngsters were trying to bite through the tremendously tough hide of the creature's legs. They were no more than annoying the beast, but as I said, it wasn't as defenseless as it looked. Its tail, thicker toward its end than our entire bodies, swung in an irresistible arc that caught three of the youngsters just as they were darting in to simultaneously attack a leg. All three hurtled through the air, and Eighteenth and Twentieth-Born did not rise when they landed. We would return to see how they fared after we found food for the rest of us, but for us to spend time with them now to see if they would recover would simply mean that we might all die of starvation. I had just grunted an end to the game we were playing with the Swamp-monster, when the second mysterious thing happened that day. I had been watching, out of the corner of my eye, a group of creatures slightly smaller than us, who in turn seemed to be watching us from the nearby hilltop. They had the two shiny-flying-creatures with them, so I knew them to be the ones we had seen earlier beside the Egg/mother. Of the Egg/mother itself, there was no sign. They stood on their hind feet, very much like one of The People, though they seemed strangely incomplete without a decent tail. They seemed to be mainly blue or tan in color, but they had particularly ugly pink faces and paws. And it almost looked like they were wearing leaves on their head.

One of the blue creatures aimed a stick at the Swamp-monster, and I saw a sudden flare of lightning-flame. That was strange, but what happened next was incredible. The abdomen of the Swamp-monster just disappeared. There was thunder without a storm, and suddenly the great beast was mortally wounded and gushing blood.

As one, the pack ran away from the terrible noise, but we stopped. The scent of life-giving blood was in the air, and the huge monster suddenly toppled onto its side. I knew from experience that it would move in its death throes for some time to come, but it was helpless. That was enough. I growled at the others to stay back, and then I investigated. As Firstborn, I had some privileges, but also the responsibility of leadership. Before the pack closed, I had to ensure that this was not some sort of trick.

The meat was real, and the beast, although it still twitched, seemed permanently down. Satisfied, I called the others in. We had an incredible feast of rich meat, and it was all ours, at least for the moment. We gorged, for we could not move or hide this carcass, and such a mountain of meat would attract those who, while stupid, had brawn that we lacked. Overhead, I could already hear the cry of the giant Flying-creatures. They were big enough to be a danger to us, but they were ungainly when they landed, and a concerted attack by the entire pack made them quite vulnerable. So we had come to a kind of agreement. They would not land until we were done, but we would feed, and then leave the vicinity of the carcass. Still, the Flying-creature's cries were bringing more of its kind, and soon there was a great circle of them riding the thermals and screaming at us to leave. They were not what I worried about. They could not seem to act in concert, so we could handle them with teamwork. It was Big-hunter that I feared. He was a pea-brain, but he had more muscles than he knew what to do with, and his jaws could bite one of the People in two with a single snap. He couldn't generally catch us, but we, in turn, could do very little to harm him. And if he got in reach of one of us, we were dead.

Even as I thought about the unhappy possibility of one of the Big-hunters coming upon the scene, I heard a deep grumble from far away. The bugling of the High-standers, who had edged their way back toward us, clinched it. There was no other pack of The People who would dare to hunt in our territory, so the approaching danger could only be Big-hunter.

Cautious, I called to Thirteenth-born, and the two of us sniffed the breeze. When that didn't satisfy our curiosity, we coursed in the Direction-of-the-Setting-Sun to see what approached. We did not have far to go. A deep roar announced the arrival of a Big-hunter. The herd animals panicked again, and stampeded across the-land-of-the-grass. Through the dust raised by the stampeding animals, I caught a glimpse of a bronze-colored creature that could only be Big-hunter. That was enough. I ran for the pack. Big-hunter is stupid, but he is not so stupid that he cannot figure out why an entire flock of giant Flying-creatures circled overhead.

The Big-hunter ignored the lesser herd beasts, and made directly for the area so kindly marked by the Flying-creatures. He did not even slow when two Spiky-horns attempted to engage him. Before he would risk combat, he clearly intended to see if he could steal another creature's catch; ours!

Well, we were sated anyway, and only hung around to annoy the giant Flying-creatures. We backed off as Big-hunter approached. He was not in the least interested in us. He knew we would not challenge his right to the carcass. He was quite right. I led the pack in the Direction-of-the-Rising-Sun. I still saw the strange creatures on the hill, and I was curious. I had never seen their like before.

I set a sedate pace, for although our bodies were now warm, our stomachs were full, and a certain lethargy came over the tribe. I led the pack, by a circular route, to a copse of trees behind the hilltop, where we would be invisible to the Stranger/creatures, but could observe them.

I was totally puzzled when they set up some sort of structures. They almost seemed to be nests, but it was not leaves and dirt that they used. They clustered around the nests, but did not even bother posting sentries. They seemed fearless, which, when you are as small as they were, seemed pretty stupid. The two Shiny-flying-creatures settled down beside them, so perhaps these beasts were there to protect them. The concept was novel, but not impossible to grasp. The Spiky-horns herded with the Tall-standers, and allowed them to act as sentries. If my idea was valid, then the little creatures obviously had a high level of intelligence.

Whoever sits on a hilltop in plain sight and does not take precautions has either got powerful protectors, or is very stupid. I was not hungry, so the question was, for the moment, quite academic. Still, the Big-hunter was not far away, and all animals were right to fear him. I knew of none who were safe from his powerful jaws, unless they could hide, or run very fast.

The evening mists rolled in, and the temperature started to drop. I could feel my own body becoming even more lethargic as my blood cooled. At least it was a time of little danger to us, as all in the animal kingdom also slowed. The only exceptions were the tiny Furry-animals. They seemed to be able to maintain their alertness, whatever the temperature. Fortunately, they were all small and helpless; barely a meal when we caught them in the heat of the day. And these Stranger/creatures. Parts of their bodies seemed to change color, but they seemed in no other way to be affected by the evening cold.

I did note, however, that they eventually all crawled into their non-leaf nests. Only the two grounded Shiny-flying-creatures remained outside. Whether they were on sentry duty or were asleep, I had no way of knowing.

I slept the good sleep of a full stomach and companionship of ones' egg-mates. I assumed that even the monster Big-hunter and the Flying-creatures could not polish off the entire carcass of the Swamp-monster, but I wasn't too sure I cared. In the evening, the Stranger/creatures had done something with meat, and the wafting wind had brought me delicious odors, mixed in with the scent of the creatures themselves. They smelled warm-blooded, and that helped to explain how they could keep moving about so easily.

I had never seen a warm-blooded animal so large before, or so stupid. They seemed to know many interesting tricks, but to nest on a hilltop with a pack of The People on one side and a Big-hunter on the other is really not smart. I debated if we should wait until the morning sun had raised our temperature enough that we could be fully active again. The odor of our guests was truly delicious. I was not sure how to cope with the Shiny-flying-creatures, but they were resting on the ground, and we would, in any case, try to avoid them. Of the Stranger/creatures, I had no worry. They were not big enough to be a threat to us. They were large enough, however, to be a tasty meal.

We basked under the early-morning sun, in a glade in the middle of the copse of woods. I eventually moved the pack close to the edge of the woods, though they were still groggy from the cold. They grumbled, but I managed to convince them of the necessity of moving early. It was not every day that such choice morsels were offered to us. Usually we had to take large risks to fill our bellies. I remembered as we moved that we had not checked on the fate of our egg-mates since Big-hunter had arrived. They had not rejoined us, though our scent trail was plain. With the giant flying-creatures circling, and Big-hunter in the vicinity, it was pretty obvious that they would not be returning.

While The People moved slowly and gradually raised their body temperatures, I took up my old position on the edge of the copse; in order to spy on the stranger-animals. My body warmed by the muscular effort. It was wasteful of energy, but I was not concerned. Our breakfast had not yet left its hilltop site, though the grassland animals had long before woken, and were beginning to stir under the warm morning sun.

At last I knew that The People would be ready for action. I loped back to where I had left them, and grunted the orders for the attack.

Half of the group followed me, and half followed Second-born. We intended to hit the site on two sides simultaneously. Our group would vocalize, while the other group would move in more slowly and silently. We would get the creatures running, and they would catch any who managed to get away from us. It was one of our favorite hunting tricks, and it almost always worked.

I bellowed loudly enough that the herd animals all lifted their heads and stared wildly about. We crossed the open ground and hit the non-leaf nests at a full gallop. Pandemonium broke out on the Land-of-the-Grass. I reached the first hilltop nest, and tore at the thin material with my claws and teeth. It tasted strange; damp and yet dry. It tore with a loud continuous noise, and I reached in. The fat one I had spotted the evening before was inside. He was now a disgusting shade of pink all over, and he squealed so loudly that it hurt my ears. I was forced to bite his head off to shut him up. His skin was soft, and he seemed to have no natural defenses. His teeth were pathetic, and he had no claws worthy of the name.

I wondered just how these creatures had survived as long as they had, and then I turned to help my egg-mates at the next nest. My egg-mates at the second non-leaf nest were in the process of having a very different experience, however. A series of short thunder-bursts greeted Ninth-born, and surprisingly, she started to stagger. Blood began to pour from a series of wounds on her chest, yet I could see that the blue creature facing her had not touched her, but merely pointed a stick at her. I then remembered what happened to the Swamp-monster. It was at that moment that I realized these creatures were far from totally helpless. Still, there were only five of them, and still seventeen of us.

I had worried most about the Shiny-flying-creatures sitting on the ground, but they remained inert. Seventh-born had even attacked one, and nothing had happened. Its thick skin seemed impervious to her teeth and claws, but by the same token, the creature did not retaliate in any way. I whistled the rest of the pack in. If the Stranger/creatures were capable of killing us one at a time, we would have to overwhelm them en masse. We would simply have to accept the casualties. In the next dry season, we would lay as many eggs as possible, and, with luck, we could build our numbers back up again. I already had my eye on Fourteenth-born. He was turning into a fine stallion. I thought that I might honor him as my mate for the season.

The three beige creatures succumbed easily to our attack. I had personally taken care of one of them. The two blue creatures were a different matter. After we tore the thunder-sticks out of their paws, they drew smaller versions of the thunder-sticks, and each wielded a single shiny claw that was much longer, and more deadly, than any we possessed. At last, however, we overwhelmed the five of them, and we feasted. We felt sadness that six of our number had been killed, but we finally finished off the last of the Stranger/creatures. I am still puzzled about the two Shiny-flying-creatures. I had feared them the most, and I had seen them travel at tremendous speed. Yet they just sat while we killed the little creatures who had ridden on their backs. Perhaps they didn't care. There was nothing left of interest, and our bellies were full. I ordered the pack to form up.

As I surveyed the nest-site one last time, I puzzled over the creatures we had eaten. They had seemed helpless, yet they killed six of our number, and could casually strike down a Swamp-monster. They were foolishly nesting on a hilltop, yet controlled creatures far greater than themselves. They carried portable nests, and could move freely in late night cold. What manner of creatures were they? Could they be a serious threat to my kind? We had no name for them, and we always named the prey animals we hunted. I decided to call them Humans.

I was always intrigued that, historically, some of the Turks' greatest regiments were composed of the children of their enemies, brainwashed and trained from childhood as Turkish Janissaries. What would happen if a ruthless alien race came across Humans scattered amongst the stars? Might they do the same? In this story, the monsters come from outer space. Man fights a magnificent fight, but the aliens use the greatest weapons of all against man - other men!

4. JANISSARY

"You! Toad! My name isss Corporal Si'isss, and, son, your cloaca belongssss to me! On your feet! You haven't got all day!"

I stare in awe at the Corporal, magnificent in his burnished green scales. He has no more time for me, however. He turns to the birthing angels in white on either side of me. "Get a move on with the processss, unlessss you want to join them!"

I can sense the fear of the two men in white coats. They rush to twirl some dials and start removing wires from my body.

As the Corporal goes by again I stare at him. He is almost twice my height, and he is a glorious sight. I look down at my arms while some cables are being disconnected, and I see a pallid pink and unarmored skin. I feel ashamed. I seem to be a fragile vessel, not worthy to be in the same room as the glorious corporal. I manage to croak out a few words.

"Honored Corporal, have I truly just been born?"

"Of courssse, toad! And you been taking a damned long time at it. As sssoon as they get the wiresss off you, you will be finally done. It isss a damned good thing, too. You were needed on the front liness daysss ago!"

"Corporal, you said the 'front lines'. Where is that and what will I do there?"

"You are a ssstupid toad! You will be given the opportunity to offer your life for the glory of the Empire of the Ssstelig."

"I am not worthy, Corporal. I see before me a magnificent specimen of manhood, while I am only a pale slug. I do not have your natural armor or teeth. Surely I am not worthy of the honor of dying for the Empire!?"

Corporal Si'isss looks momentarily pleased. I can see row after row of powerful pointed teeth in his powerful jaw. "I look that way to you becaussse I am a member of the Ssstelig race. Your kind hasss good reflexesss, however, and, in massss waves, you are moderately effective.

Now hurry up! Mossst of your sssquad have already finisssshed birthing. They wait outsssside."

I let myself swell with the honor of being a chosen warrior for the Ssstelig, then I force my mind to take command of my lethargic body. Gradually I gain control over my legs . . . An errant thought flashes through my mind. How do I know that those limbs are called legs? . . . and then my arm and hands. With shaking fingers I undo the last straps that hold me to the Gurney, and the angels in white hurry to remove the last electrodes from my bare skull.

I stagger erect, and Si'isss nods curtly. "Here isss

clothing. Cover your disssgussting body immediately!"

I look down at my pale skin, and I am ashamed again. I shrug quickly into the clothes Si'isss has thrust at me with his third and fourth arms. I wonder if I have done this before. I seem to instinctively know what to do, and quickly figure out the mystery of the clothes fastenings. Within moments I am dressed and standing at attention. Si'isss talks abruptly to the next figure on a Gurney, but then deigns to notice me.

"About time, toad! Now get your cloaca out that door and join the formassion!"

When I pause to ask a further question, my head suddenly explodes with pain. I run blindly for the door, and the pain eases. I will remember next time. 'Do what you're told, without hesitation!'

Outside there are more pink uniformed slugs like myself. I fall in at the end of the line and stand rigidly at attention. I do not know why I know to do this, but I do. The knowledge I need in my new life seems to flow into my head as I need it.

Corporal Si'isss finally arrives with the last birthing stragglers, and he leads us off at a brisk pace. As the formation moves over the purple grass and into the shelter of brown-leaved trees, I have an attack of deja vu. I am somewhere else, and the trees are an impossible shade of green. Instead of an orange sky, I see a clear blue one! I shake my head, trying to physically dislodge my waking dream. I concentrate on moving my body with absolute precision, hoping that I can leave the disturbing vision behind.

I wake quickly, eager to get back to training. The chow-line is moving, so I join the slowly snaking line of men. It's gruel again; my favorite. I stand close to the guy in front of me, but he doesn't say anything, and neither do I. Corporal Si'isss says there is no sense in getting too friendly with your squad mates. He says that it will just be harder to leave them behind when they get hurt.

His brilliant words are drilled into my consciousness. "You will leave injured men where they fall. Whole battles have been lossst because a toad foolisssly ssstopped to help sssome guy who isss going to die anywaysss. Look, toadsss. Thisss is the coup-de-grassse cut for the wounded. A quick slissse, and your wounded companion isss out of pain forever."

I bolt my chow, and am left with a few minutes of time before formation. I make my bed and wash my face and hands. Cleanliness is next to Godliness, or so Corporal Si'isss tells us.

I am excited when the bugle call for formation finally blows. The two suns are in a low line, parallel with the horizon. It's the signal for our working day to begin.

I am awed that Corporal Si'isss is willing to spend time with us. We all work hard, and within days I can kill a pink slug with thirty-seven different blows. I can strip a blaster right down to its component pieces and have it back in working order in less than a minute. After steroid treatment, my skin goes all blotchy and I feel constant pain, but Corporal Si'isss says it is a small price to pay for the increased strength. I find myself able to run for twenty crocoids without pausing, and after that I can pull myself up a cliff using my hands alone.

I may be only a shadow of Corporal Si'isss, but I learn that I will be fighting creatures that look a lot like me. Corporal Si'isss tells us, however, that they took a wrong turn somewhere in their evolution. Mere mammals like me, they first foolishly colonized planets before the Ssstelig reached them, and then had the audacity to refuse to vacate them in the face of the Ssstelig arrival.

Hundreds, thousands of us, as soon as we are finished training, are to be rushed to the front. Corporal Si'isss' immortal words ring in my head. "The Human toads must be stopped, at any cost. The future livesss of millionsss of unborn Ssstelig hatchlingsss depend on you!"

Our training is completed within another week, and Corporal Si'isss himself deigns to inspect us. We stand rigidly at attention.

"You have done well.' This is the first time Corporal Si'isss has ever said a good word to any of us. I can feel the pride flow up and down the ranks. 'You are all moving to the front tomorrow morning. The Humansss have launched a new offensssive, and you will be expected to ssstop them! There will be no excussses for failure! Remember, you were trained by the best Corporal in the army. Remember, too, that the greatessst glory you can achieve isss to die for the Empire of the Ssstelig."

In my excitement, I commit a cardinal sin. I speak out without permission. "Corporal, are you not coming with us?"

To my surprise I am not chastised. "I cannot, little toad. I have not been given the honor. I have been inssstructed to ssstay and train the next birthing classss. Go forth, my brave onesss, and make me proud! You are all real Janisssariesss now!"

We are thrown into the battle almost immediately. Hovertanks slide towards us, while clusters of enemy infantrymen creep up behind them. We see them coming, and we are ready.

The tanks look awesome, but they are actually easy to take care of. While we attract the infantrymen's attention with a few shots and then we pull back, a couple of the squad members hide in the tall grass. When the tank got close, they slide underneath and fire the shaped charges strapped to their bellies. The enemy infantry race up, but there isn't anybody left to kill, and another human tank has already bit the dust.

I am dug in just behind the crest of the hill, and we are told to hold the humans at all costs. We scythe them as they are silhouetted on the crest. Our gun barrels glow red hot, but nothing alive makes it down our side of the hill.

The human bastards start dropping some heavy stuff on us, but we just take the casualties. They can't break us, and eventually they are forced to withdraw. I stand at the top of the hill and watch them retreat. My chest puffs out with pride when I see that. I hope that Corporal Si'isss would be proud of me and the guys.

Corporal Se'esss points out the men he wants. "You. You. And you. Follow me. You have jussst volunteered for a little reconnaissance patrol."

Being the third 'you', I follow the big bull into the forest.

We walk a couple of dozen crocoids, and then the Corporal holds his third arm up to signal a halt. He waves us to join him, and we rush to obey. He keeps his voice low, but we hang on to every word he says.

"Just beyond thossse treesss there isss an isssolated farmhoussse. You will move in and take the humansss living there captive. You!'

The corporal points again at me. 'When all isss sssecure, you will report to me here. Questionsss?"

We all shake our heads.

"Good. Janissssariesss, move out!"

The attack goes pretty-much according to plan. The three of us slither up fairly close, but we spread out so we have three separate arcs of fire.

We do not have long to wait for some action. The screen door slams suddenly, and an immature human comes out of the building carrying a bucket of grain. My rifle leaps to my shoulder almost without thought, but then I remember our orders. We are to take captives here, not kill. My finger eases off the firing stud.

I watch the small human scatter grain on the ground. Soon it is the center of a whirlwind of activity as an entire herd of feathered creatures flutter around it's skirts.

The door opens a second time, and I am again sighting the gun without conscious thought. The creature that comes out next is puzzling. It seems human, but its shape is all wrong. The hair flows over shoulders that seem too narrow, and the chest protrudes in a most disturbing way. I have killed a lot of humans, but have not seen one that looks like this. And yet, and yet . . . the shape is tantalizing familiar.

I find myself wanting to see the creature naked. It is more than casual curiosity, however. My pisser stirs in a most unnatural way.

As I lie in the bushes, I imagine touching those strange protrusions, and then another haunting memory slips uninvited into my mind. Suddenly I am naked with a . . . a woman! My hands slide over her breasts, and she moans.

I shake my head. I know beyond a shadow of a doubt that a male fertilizes it's mate's eggs only after the female has laid them. There is no need . . . no desire . . . for disgusting physical proximity. If I know that to be a certainty, from where is my mind dredging up these strange memories?

I battle the waking nightmares with action. I charge forward, rifle at the ready. The woman freezes. My two companions, seeing me break cover, run to the door and burst through. Moments later a male, his face bloody, is dragged out to join his female.

After we ensure that there is no further danger, I run back and retrieve Corporal Se'esss. He surveys the little family, and smiles a smile that exposes his hundreds of sharp teeth.

"Well done, little toadsss!"

He inspects the man most minutely. "A puny specimen, but we can probably make a janissssary of him."

The Corporal turns to me. "Kill thossse two. We will

take the male with us."

As I raise the rifle, the girl starts screaming at me in a language I do not understand. Then, suddenly, I do. As her shrill little words echo in my head, I see my own wife falling as an energy burst burns her in two.

A green monster grabs my little boy and bashes in his head in with a single sickening blow. I attack my wife's killer with a rock and my bare fists, but the monster just twists my arm and scornfully disarms me. The last I remember is a clout to my head, and then, and then . . . I woke up in the birthing place.

I look at the woman in front of me. My head hurts terribly, and the rifle pauses. What kind of evil creature have I become?!

Suddenly I know that two suns are an abomination. Grass is green, and the sky should be blue! I am living a nightmare, but it is real.

I remember the stories then. Earth and several of its colonies across several light-years had been attacked by a terrible foe. Millions of citizens on defenseless planets were seized and abducted. No one knew what had happened to all the victims. Now I know. More are 'birthing' even as I stand by the lonely farmhouse.

I whirl with the rifle. Somewhere behind me is a monster.

I am too slow. Even as the rifle comes around, a giant claw thuds against my head.

"You! Toad! My name isss Corporal Si'isss, and, ssson, your cloaca belongssss to me! Hurry up, you haven't got all day!"

I stare in awe at the Corporal, magnificent in his burnished green scales.

**Long, long ago, on a dark and stormy
night, my mind wandered far from my
assignments. Write a term paper, read a
boring text book, or ride my fantasy into
deepest space. The choice was a no-
brainer. I strapped on my trusty blaster
and went looking for the villain. Even in
the empire of the future, good lawmen
were needed. Here is a space western,
lovingly re-written many times - a story
from my university days.**

5. IN THE NAME OF THE LAW

A flaming needle of light split the tranquil skies over
Fawcett. The peaceful inhabitants looked up from the
roads and fields at the strange unscheduled arrival of a
deep space cruiser.

Like a great metal falcon, the lean cruiser hurtled
ground ward in a power dive. Then, like the falcon drawn
to its lure, it settled gently to the ground.

Men and women from miles around, dressed in
coarse homespun and wide-brimmed hats, saddled up
their esquits. All six legs pounding, the beasts were
directed to head for the spaceport. An event as
momentous as this could scarcely be ignored. Work was
forgotten as neighbor joined neighbor on the ride to the
star base.

It did not take long for the people to discover the
reason for the unscheduled visit. Down the ramp of the

cruiser marched an evil and brutal group. It was a bird-of-prey indeed that visited the farm planet of Fawcett, but not the lordly falcon.

Instead, it was the avaricious vulture. Even in the rustic stillwater of Fawcett, people recognized the notorious 'Varell' Quint. His somber black outfit and muscular frame, coupled with his sallow face and blazing eyes, only served to accentuate the gleaming twin Varells slung low on his hips. Behind him ranged his human jackals.

Even the smallest child knew and feared what his arrival meant. It had been in 2578 A.D. that the legal system of Terra, transplanted to all the planets of her empire, finally crumpled. The sheer distance of outer space meant that, on the rapidly expanding fringes of the Empire, avarice and greed fought and defeated the triplicate copies of justice.

A man could cross the galaxy before a warrant for his arrest could be countersigned, duplicated, and shunted across the Empire. Thus in that momentous year, the decision that saved the Empire was formulated.

Citizens lost their right to demand an arrest warrant issued from Terra. Instead, brave men were recruited as Enforcers. Armed with guts and Varell flamers, single Enforcers shot it out with vicious bandits. There were no legal appeals from a Varell flamer. The energy beams left nothing but cinders and charred flesh.

Forced to fight or perish, the fringe killers found that justice and right eventually won. Justice was suddenly swifter, and much more deadly. The number of criminals plummeted. Others fled.

Varell Quint was one of the latter. His lightning hands burned down his share and more of Enforcers, but the minions of justice kept coming. Varrell had decided to re-locate. Deserting the Fringes, he looked inward, to the rich and settled provinces.

Now, as on a half-hundred other hapless planets, he came to demand tribute. No one knew better than he that peaceful agricultural planets were unable to field a single good duelist. Hundreds of years of peace and prosperity, deep within the Empire, had made Fawcett soft. Thus, by legal Right of Duel, Quint could claim whatever struck his fancy. The law of the Empire was quite clear. In case of legal disagreement, champions were chosen, who met in single combat. Quint, however, counted on the fact there was no Enforcer on Fawcett capable of credibly representing the side of law and justice.

The entire constabulary of the planet perished in the blinding flash of pure focused light. The people watched their fat and beloved deputy Enforcer, whose gun had not left its holster in twenty years, writhe and die as Quint's practiced hands casually flamed the man down.

After one exhibition of Quint's talent, few dared challenge him to legal duel. The jackals ran rampant. Under Quint's bloodshot eyes, many of the simple treasures the people possessed were demanded and seized. Two or three of the younger, more daring youths, refused to submit meekly. Their charred remains were borne home to grief-stricken parents.

It was only hours before the scavenger cruiser was set to lift off. Annie Dodds was foolish enough to rush out from her family's pickle cellar to help defend her mother's scant belongings, threatened by ravaging human vultures whose gun-arms, though not comparable with their master's, were still as deadly to peaceful farmers as a coiled Terran Fer-de-Lance.

Instantly, she, and not the ancient silver candlestick, became the center of attraction. With practiced efficiency, she was electro-cuffed and trundled off with the other valuables.

The town was stunned. For over two hundred years,

no one had ever broken an Imperial decree. Psychologically, they were incapable of forming an avenging posse without the official sanction of Terra. But kidnapping was beyond the Code of Dueling. Kidnapping, being Illegal, roused the populace to a fury they could not otherwise have reached when it was just goods that were in dispute. The vultures had crossed the line. Nevertheless, the peoples' fury was impotent.

As the church bell summoned all the adults of Fawcett City to an emergency meeting, 'Varell's vultures' openly mixed with the crowd and smirked.

The mayor was speaking. "Is there none here who has enough guts to stand up to these... these barbarians?! Is there not one amongst you who would be our champion?"

He was almost incoherent with emotion as he spoke. The young men hung their heads and scowled furiously at the ground. One of the vultures calmly demanded, and got, the mayor's prized-heirloom gold pocket watch.

Finally a feeble voice rang out from the rear of the throng. "I hereby issue a challenge to this Varell fellow. I will stand for justice!"

Even the townspeople couldn't help but laugh derisively as the old man hobbled painfully to the front. The vultures were even good enough to offer their flamers, and to help the old man strap them on.

One Lieutenant, between convulsions of laughter, finally managed to signal Quint on his wrist communicator. The old man refused all offers of assistance, but stated in his cracked old voice that he would meet Quint in front of the Town Hall in twenty minutes. Quint, via the communicator, laughingly agreed.

The crowd was thick. Except for the aisle left for the lethal beams, and the two contestants, the street was packed. Quint stood impatiently, in a hurry to kill the old fool, and then lift off-planet.

The door of the Town Hall opened, and from its shadow stepped a black shape to face the black-dressed killer. The dress of the two men were similar, except that the old man wore a tall white feather in his hat band. More ominously, his twin Varells were jet black. Everyone gasped. Even Quint's sallow face paled. The vultures tried unobtrusively to slip into the crowd and disappear.

Such a white feather and black Varells were known throughout the Empire. They were the trade mark of the fastest man ever known. Given status of First Enforcer, for over twenty years he had been a law unto himself. He had been personally chosen to represent the Emperor himself, and in this task he had never once failed. More, his Varells had been instrumental in breaking the criminal hold on the far-flung Rim. Then, some twenty-five years before, he had disappeared.

It had been rumored that the First Enforcer craved anonymity and retirement. No one knew! And a quick check with the planetary data-bank indicated that it was twenty four years since a space tramp had left the old man, independently wealthy, on Fawcett.

The old man walked forward confidently. Gone was his limp. His bent back was straight, and his hands hovered menacingly over his pistol butts.

Quint's hands climbed slowly higher, far from his holstered weapons. "Maybe I was wrong about you, old timer. Maybe we could let the girl go."

Already his hands were as high as his neck, and still rising in the universal gesture of surrender.

The old man spoke, no longer in his old whine.

"Do you officially surrender, then?"

Quint stared for long seconds. His courage wilted. Finally he whined "Okay, but don't shoot!"

"Then in the name of . . ."

Quint's hand slapped his hidden neck holster and a long slim flamer leapt into his waiting hand. He flung it out at lightening speed, and pressed the firing stud. To the left of the old man, molten asphalt flowed.

The old man's twin guns came up slowly, deliberately. Almost casually, he pressed his firing studs. The sickening stench of Quint's charred body wafted slowly through the crowd. Most just stood and stared at the man who had killed the Killer.

".... Jesus Christ, our Savior, I ask God to forgive you your evil deeds."

The mayor finally spoke.

"Do you mean you weren't going to arrest him before he grabbed his flamer?"

The old man hobbled painfully over towards the mayor. "Don't be silly, Mayor. I don't have any authority for that. Now help me get the shoe polish off these damn old guns. I gotta return them to a friend."

It was almost 11 PM at Acadia University in bucolic downtown Wolfville, and I still had a couple of hours of homework left to do. My pen wandered to a blank sheet of paper. This story was struggling to get out. What to do? Study or procrastinate? That night, this story was born.

6. MANS' BEST FRIEND

The young couple spent hours at the Louvre. Arm in arm, they walked the endless corridors, pausing now and again to admire the magnificent works of art.

"Which one do you like the best, my love?" The man whispered, as he nuzzled her mate's ear.

"I think, mmm, maybe the Mona Lisa. I find her expression fascinating. What about you? If you had millions of credits, which one would you take home?"

"If you like the Mona Lisa, then that's the one! Of course, we would have to rob a credit center. That or we could try and hide it in your bra!"

"Ya, right! You're just looking for an excuse to get my bra off!"

"If the truth were known, it's not your bra that I want to get off."

She hit him a playful punch. "You men are all alike!"

"Hey, don't get mad at me! I'm programmed to be attracted to your magnificent assets. The guys at the factory did a good job on me."

She swung another punch at him. "You just see that you keep your hands off my ass-sets, mister!"

"Come, my love! Show some decorum, or the security guards will throw us out of here. We don't want rumors about ugly Americans to sweep the city!"

"Now you're calling me ugly! Mister, you are in such trouble! Just you wait until I get you back in our room!"

"Always promises! Since that really big, beefy security type is heading our way, however, let's just pretend that we are just innocent American tourists on our very first European tour. See that you behave accordingly."

Finally, exhausted, the couple traveled back by metro to the vicinity of the Eiffel Tower, where they had found a reasonably priced small pension which catered to foreign tourists. Exiting the subway, the male looked in both directions for a taxi.

She smiled at him. "Darling, it's so beautiful. What do you say we walk back to the hotel? I don't think it's far from here. And the cabs are so dirty and so expensive.' She tugged at his arm. 'Come on, you ol' stick-in-the mud!"

"Well, it is still light out, and our debit card can't take too many more unexpected hits. Sure, why not? It is decided, Madame. We walk! - Ah, do you know exactly where the pension is, my love?"

"Of course, my handsome hunk. I have a compass hard-wired into my brain."

She grinned suddenly. "Besides, we just head for that great pile of steel over there."

"Pile of steel! You will single-handedly start those rumors of ugly American again! That 'pile of steel'. is the unique and world-renowned symbol of Paris!"

As they walked, the sun slowly dipped towards the western horizon. Each block brought them new and interesting sights. They marveled at the beauty and antiquity of the varied buildings. Most had been built more than two hundred years previously, had stood empty for the over eighty years since the 'Liberation', and yet they stood as proudly as the day they were completed.

The two stopped as they hit an intersection that gave them a view to the west. "Darling, look how low the sun is. It truly is setting. The concierge at the pension said that these streets can be really dangerous after dark. Maybe we should look for a cab, after all."

"Don't you, worry, dearest!' She playfully flexed her biceps. 'I have muscles of steel. I'll protect you!"

In spite of her levity, however, they lengthened their pace. As they hurried in the dwindling light, they came to an alley."

He turned to her. "Finally, my love. I was getting worried. This is the alley we used this very morning. It takes us directly to the back door, which will save us having to detour several blocks."

She looked anxiously at him. "Do you think it's safe?"

"I don't know, but it'll be completely dark if we go the other way. This way is at least faster."

"OK, love. Let's do it!"

As the couple entered the darkened alley, they heard scuffling noises. Suddenly, their path was blocked. They stared wildly around, only to see the savage and snarling faces of a wild pack. They had been told that when the sun set, the wild packs ruled the alleys. These animals dared to wear rags over their genitals, and their necks were devoid of collars-of-ownership. The two lovers trembled and moved closer together. They backed against the stone wall. The pack members bared their teeth and moved steadily forward. They had a healthy respect for the strength and speed of their intended victims. Each of the members of the pack carried, however, a metal pipe or rod.

Accepting that confrontation was inevitable, the male stepped in front of his partner. He was ready to defend her with his life against the wild animals ranged before him.

"Come on, you bastards. See if you're good enough to take me on!"

"Be careful, dear! Push the alarm!"

Belatedly, the male pressed the alarm button on his chrono. The signal, relayed to three geosynchronous satellites above, would both instantly locate him to within several feet, and alert the local gendarmes that he was in danger.

The pack showed animal cunning. They seemed aware that one of their victims had signaled for help, yet they continued to advance deliberately and in a loose formation. The arc of attackers feinted forwards and backwards, and constantly shifted from side to side

The tourist was able to deflect a powerful w of a metal rod with his forearm. In spite of the shock to his arm, he was able to grab and hold on to the rod. He was seconds from wrestling it from the animal who wielded it, when a heavy pipe smashed against the inside of his knee. He collapsed. Instantly a half dozen pipes and rods rose and fell. He was given no chance to recover.

Ululating sirens in the distance indicated that help was on its way, but the wild pack didn't even pause. They turned and moved towards the female who now stood alone against the building. The pack steadily closed on her.

One of their number was caught in a grip of steel and hurled with irresistible force against the wall, but the rest used the opportunity to strike with their improvised weapons. She screamed in terror and pain, and collapsed under the savage onslaught.

The two bodies lay inert, battered almost beyond recognition. Even the alloy bones were twisted, and the tough plastic skin was savagely torn open. The pack leader uttered a guttural call, and the pack stepped back. Machine oil stained the pavement in an ever-widening pool. The savage animals, amongst the last free humans on Earth, loped away; down the alley way built by their ancestors.

For me, there are few better escapes from the stress of work and life in general than my pen - okay, actually my word processor. For a few hours at a time I escape into the past or the future. I have written several novels set in the future, and an entire historical series. I have only ever written one story set in the present. When an idea lurches out of my sub-conscious, my eyes glaze over and I shamefully ignore my loving family. For a few hours, reality only intrudes gently and the pressures of work are far away.

7. SHADES OF POCAHONTAS

"Some nights I would camp out on the southern shore and gaze north toward the city across the river. I could see the glowing lights even from that distance. They lit up the sky so that there was a glow that partly obscured the stars. It always seemed incredible that the city folk had so much power to burn that they could do that.

Sometimes I even saw a jump-jet descend from the heavens. I would see great towers of flame supporting it as it gently dropped below my horizon. I was awed. I know the theory of how planes fly, but it always struck me as incredible that such a big piece of metal could land as lightly as a feather. I often lay on the beach and dreamed that someday I might actually fly in one of those giant metal birds.

It was safe enough to cross the river, although I was always nervous when I was out on its open waters. I felt helpless and vulnerable; my canoe paddle against all the advanced technology the mysterious city folk could conjure up.

In spite of all their vaunted science and hydroponics, however, the city dwellers apparently still needed to supplement their food supplies. Thus they had need of us 'hewers of wood and drawers of water', whatever that meant. It was a line I took from one of the three precious books that resided splendiferously in our school room. I'm not sure what that means either, but my teacher liked the word a lot.

The western tip of the island was not fenced against us. A special market had been set up on the ruins of a college where once hundreds of students had studied and partied. The Townies let us land there to sell our fresh produce.

Sometimes they brought their families to gawk at us as we squatted in the dirt and tried to bargain with them. Armed young bucks kept an eye on us, and when we grew too obstreperous, a couple of the thugs would beat the seller unconscious.

Such were the financial constraints of our little market. We had no chance to follow the Townie vehicles back into the City territory however, because just to the east stretched a gate and the first of the barricades that were designed to keep us out of their precious city.

The fence itself was relatively innocuous, being not more than three meters in height and made of wire mesh. The lethal voltage that surged through it was by itself not a serious deterrent to the younger and more adventurous amongst us. A shovel, a long pole, or an overhanging tree easily neutralized its feeble defense.

The fence was only meant to be symbolic, however. There was almost a kilometer of open land on the other side, after which there was a second fence, and another gate. The open land was the real defense. As incautious villagers had found to their family's great sorrow, the Townies had a variety of other perimeter defense systems.

Armed human patrols were infrequent, but randomly timed. Francois, our village smithy and electronics genius, had come with me to the Trading Gate once, and he easily identified several electronic systems. He told me about infrared and seismic sensors, motion and electrical field detectors.

He said he wasn't sure, but he figured that there might be other systems also, that he didn't know about. In any event, any intrusion into the open area brought a rapid response from Eyespies.

The glass and metal balls floated on anti-gravs. It seemed to me that they were the eyes of the defense system, and more. Under each Eyespy hung an energy or projectile weapon.

We enjoyed tossing rabbits over the fence when no Townies were present. Within seconds after they started scampering across the open ground, one or two Eyespies would appear from the east and quickly vector in on them. A burst of flame or metal ended their lives mercifully quickly. We used to put bets on which one would be flamed first.

I suspect it made the Townies annoyed that we would play with their defenses, but it was also a powerful lesson to us. Each of the village children was brought, when they were old enough to make the journey, and given a demonstration.

For most, the lesson was plain. For a few like me, it was a challenge. Francois tried to dissuade me, but when it became obvious to him that I was going in with or without his help, he gave in and agreed to help me. He actually grew quite enthusiastic. I think he saw it as a challenge to his skills.

At first I was baffled that the Townies could cross the security strip in complete safety, when even a small rabbit only survived for seconds. I noticed that the Townies all wore similar necklaces, however, and my comment twigged Francois on to the trick.

The next time I made the journey to the Trading Gate, he came along. He brought some of his precious electronic equipment. He kept it well hidden from the armed goons who watched over the trading, but I could see a triumphant look cross his face when he fiddled with his bundle. I could hardly restrain myself, but I forced myself to wait until we were both in the canoe and back on the river.

"Francois, you looked like you swallowed chocolate! Just what did you find out?"

"Just keep paddling, boy! You want to go through the rapids down river?" I knew when to move the paddle instead of my mouth. I shut up and stroked.

At last he relented however, and gave me a great grin.' It's simple, 'petit chou'! Each one of the Townies was broadcasting a radio signal. Each seemed to have a unique signal, so I suspect that it is an electronic ID. Warplanes used to do that back in the Twentieth Century. An Eyespy could just check its data banks and not only identify friend or foe, but even know precisely who is there."

"Merde! That's that, then!"

"Not so fast, 'petit chou'! Let me make a transmitter, and we will send in a special bunny the next time we visit."

It took a few tries, but eventually he licked the problem. After that, the Eyespies was easy. The Townies were dumb. Just because we didn't have their precious fusion power, and were locked out of their stinkin' cities, they thought we were illiterate. Francois showed my people how to build a dam across the stream that bisected our village, and we had always had electricity, 'cept of course when the water levels were low, or the stream froze in winter.

Our smithy might not have been good enough for the Townies, but as far as I was concerned, he was a genius with electronics and 'puters. He had made me a dandy little ID scrambler, and we put it on a bunny. It kept randomly changing ID's, and the stupid Eyespies got all confused. Every once and awhile the scrambler would hit a valid ID, and that confused the hell of the stupid little electronic brains. They just floated overhead, an easy target for a quarrel dart.

Once I put a metal quarrel into 'em, they just short-circuited and flopped on the ground. Sometimes, when I had the inclination, I would cart home the pieces. Francois would take it apart and disconnect the flamer. The flamers were neat to play with, until the cells ran down. What they did to the bushes I aimed them at, though, sure made me grateful that Francois's ID scrambler worked!

What we figured out after a few experiments and quite a few dead bunnies, was that the multiple sensor system could not be bypassed. That was not the big problem that it at first had seemed, however, because an alarm signal was apparently downloaded to an automated computer system that reacted by sending out an Eyespy or two. There seemed to be no human follow-up. I guess that they thought we could never defeat their precious alarm system.

They were right. I could, however, beat their Eyespies. The first few times I shot one down, I fled under the fence and waited in hiding for some massive retaliation. Nothing ever happened. Francois guessed that the Eyespies had a limited life span, and it was probably easier for them to just replace them than to go look for the ones that ran out of fuel when out on patrol. I liked his thinking!

I had just made my deepest penetration yet, to an area of pleasant fields and scattered woods, when I heard a vehicle approaching. I lay very still in a poison sumac bush, but when I finally peeked, all I saw was a girl driving a wheeled contrivance. She had turned off the road not far from where I lay, and, being slightly suicidal, I decided to see what she was up to.

I crawled very slowly, and cautiously, through the brush. I could hear splashing nearby, and, parting some branches, I found a deep pond hidden in a glade. It was beautiful. Even more magnificent, however, was what was in the pond.

Her skin was smooth and golden in color, and her hair hung down straight and lustrous. She was young, and beautiful. She looked solid, not emaciated like our village girls. I could barely see her breasts through the underbrush, but they looked sweet. I wanted to take them in my hands and cup them like little innocent birds.

Though I had never managed to convince one of our village girls to show me her privates, I had peeked at some of them when they had gone skinny-dipping. None of our girls had looked like this! They had been deep brown where the sun had burned them, and a sickly white on the rest of their bodies.

A stirring of my own private parts told me that I actually wanted to do more to this one than just cup her sweet little golden breasts, and yet the thought seemed sacrilegious. She was so beautiful, and innocent, as she happily splashed in the shallows.

Her movements sent her breasts swinging, and I was entranced. I wanted nothing more than to part the bushes and join her. I fantasized that she would look up in surprise and then ask me to join her in her little pond.

Down deep I knew better, however. Not only would I probably be nothing more than an uncouth barbarian to my new goddess, but she might be a mite unhappy that I caught her in her birthday suit. My kind were evermore banned from the Cities; outcasts from civilization.

I knew it had not always been so. Once, or so old Pierre, the village story teller, told us, we had all lived together in a vast country called Democracy. We had all been equal, and could actually decide if we wanted to live in the country or in the city.

Pierre told us that a great plague called Crime swept over the world, and the city folk built fences and hired guards to protect themselves from this plague. Those of us unfortunate enough to have been on the outside when the fences went up were hereafter forbidden to enter the very cities that had once belonged to all of us!

Once my great grandparents may have lived in this very city, but I was a pariah. I had a pretty good idea how the girl would react if I pushed the bushes aside. Worse, I was deep in forbidden territory. A word from her would bring human forces I could not hope to outwit.

I ignored the stirring in my loins. I hunched down in the bushes, and allowed only my eyeballs to move. Better a little discomfort from the local insect denizens than a chase from armed goons who couldn't be too far away. I had little doubt what they would do to me if they caught me.

At last she stepped from the water. She toweled herself dry before she slipped into brief pants and a halter-top. I cursed the intervening branches bushes and tree trunks that blocked my view! Yet to move might have been fatal, and I was not stupid.

As the beautiful and mysterious girl walked away from the pond toward where she had left her motorized contrivance, I started to crawl away from the pond so I could put some distance between us. The last thing I wanted was for her to spot me now. The Eyespies were a less-than-subtle hint of how they treated interlopers. After I had spent twenty minutes watching my goddess bathe, I suspected that she might get a little cranked at me. I was crawling along happily on my hands and knees, when suddenly there was a rustling from the same bushes I had been so recently residing in. I looked for the source, when suddenly the face of a young man was framed in the bushes. He was doing up the belt of his trousers, and also crawling out of the bushes away from the girl. Unfortunately for me, however, he had spotted me.

"You! Boy! Stand with your hands above your head!"

I declined his foolish invitation, and immediately rolled to the right where the vegetation was densest. For a moment I wished I had kept the flamer from the last Eyespy I had shot down. I wondered if I would have actually used it.

The stranger had no such qualms. I kept rolling to the right, and he continued to incinerate the vegetation which I had only just barely vacated. Worst of all, from my perspective, he laid off trying to roast me long enough to pull out a communicator and shout into it.

I considered using a crossbow quarrel on him, if I could just reach a place where I was safe from his extravagant use of energy. I never did have the opportunity to find out if I could kill him, however, as within a minute three flying vehicles of some sort arrived.

I was by then out of his direct path-of-fire, but the number of bushes where I could hide was diminishing rapidly, thanks to his unbridled enthusiasm. I watched the crews unpack some serious-looking weapons, and decided that discretion was the better part of velour.

I called out that I would be pleased to come out for a chat, if they would just get the guy to let his flamer cool down a little. They smilingly agreed, and I stood with my hands above my head.

I had really wondered if they would just burn me on the spot, but they didn't. They fastened my hands and legs together, and then they hoisted me into the back of one of their strange vehicles. Well, I had always wanted a ride in one of their contrivances. I got one that day.

The goons tied me securely to a chair, and then physically carried me to a large and empty hall. I recognized a couple of them. The tall dark one was the one who beat Marie Claude senseless the summer before. After she lay still, he had kicked her hard several times in the ribs.

Cracking jokes at my expense, they dropped me none-too-gently on to the floor, and then left. Not having a lot to do, I let my eyes explore the room. Tables were set up across one end, but I seemed to be the only occupant for the time being.

Suddenly, however, a curtain parted, and a beautiful girl entered. I even recognized her with her clothes on. My goddess walked over to me, and I stared at her. I could not help myself. Seemingly beyond conscious control, my eyes scanned her from head to toe. Now she blushed.

"That is the second time that I have been exposed to your gaze. At least this time I have my clothes on! What is your name, boy?"

"My name is Jean Forge, and I am really sorry if I upset you today! I had no idea that you would be in the pond. I swear I did not go there to look at you, pretty lady."

"I don't know if it matters, but I believe you. My name is not 'pretty lady'. It is Pocahontas."

"Forgive me for asking, Pocahontas, but I could not help but notice that all of the people I have seen have the same reddish-gold skin that you do. We do not seem to be of the same race. I had understood that you Townies and my people were originally one."

"The answer to your question is simple. The People of the City are mainly descendants of the Iroquois and other North American Indian tribes."

"But how can that be?"

"That the savages are in the Protected City and the 'white-eyes' are fenced out?"

"That is not what I meant!"

"It doesn't matter. And the answer is simple. Once we lived to the west and south of this city. With the connivance of the 'white-eyes', your ancestors, our reservations were truncated by roads and railways. Later came bridges and a canal.

What little land we had that was not stolen by the Church or the state was poisoned by noxious effluents and acid rain. When the great plague called Separatism hit the land, the last of the Anglos fled the City. Meantime, the government tried to get out of its financial pledges to us by giving us the City gambling casinos to run, and offering us a choice of abandoned apartments.

Many of my ancestors finally abandoned the pathetic patches of land that they had fought for and scrambled to hold on to for over two hundred years. We moved to the city. Soon thereafter the walls went up around major cities around the world. This time, however, we were on the inside.

When the Protected Cities formalized the pact that allowed us to hold common citizenship in any of the member cities, many of the Francophone citizens moved south to warmer climates. My Indian ancestors, those who had managed to get into other Protected Cities around North America, chose to move here. Thus, our city population is mainly made up of First Nations people . . . what you would call North American Indians."

I was fascinated by the girl, her conversation, and her

physical beauty, but we were suddenly interrupted by the arrival of a group of older men I took to be the Elders. With them were some of the young thugs who had so recently tested the theory of gravity with my body.

As I was still tied to the chair. I concluded that they wanted me to remain for the discussion. I was not surprised to discover that I was to be the major topic of conversation.

Pocahontas' brother, who called himself Peter, and who had originally spotted me, got to speak first.

"As I approached the pond, I saw this vermin crawling through the brush away from the water. The little bastard was spying on Pocahontas! He saw her naked!

I ask my father and the Elders to let me take him outside, where I will separate him from his manhood. Then I will take him to the incinerator. If he apologizes, he can go in dead. If he doesn't, then he can feel the heat of hell before he leaves this world!"

Pocahontas stomped her feet angrily. "As if you have not gone to the pond and watched girls bathe, brother of mine! I heard you brag just last month how big Turtle Dove's nipples were. Just how would you know? In fact, why were you coming up on the pond on the only side where I couldn't see you approaching? Were you also coming to spy on your own little sister?"

Peter blushed five shades of red. "What I was doing or not doing is not relevant here! This boy has dishonored you and all of your family. He must be made to pay. It is our way."

"Father, and learned Elders! This boy was exploring an area he had never seen before. He came across an unexpected sight. I suspect he enjoyed staring at me, and I am a little embarrassed. But it's my body that he 'dishonored', and I do not wish to file a complaint. I ask you, here and now, not to punish him because of any transgressions against me."

Peter spoke again. "I will reluctantly accept Pocahontas' decision, though I cannot agree with it, yet, that settled, we still have to deal with the very serious issue of a dangerous person who has somehow evaded all of our electronic defenses. To allow him to live would be to negate the only defense we have against the outer world.

For this crime, and this crime alone, I say he should be tortured until he tells us just how he got past all of our perimeter defenses. If he cooperates fully with us, then we can let him have a painless death.

May I respectfully remind you all that for two hundred years, no one has made it through our outer perimeter. We must know how he managed it. Where there is one invader, there will be more. Our very lives depend on us discovering his secret."

Having spoken so convincingly, Peter threw a triumphant look at Pocahontas, and sat down.

Their father rose with immense dignity, and spoke next. "What Peter says is true. There is a great danger here that must be dealt with. We are a merciful people, yet our very survival could be threatened if our defenses can be so easily circumvented. I say that the Elders must give this serious thought."

Pocahontas spoke again. "Father, you said yourself that we need new blood, new genetic material, or we are going to suffer the fate of a community completely inbred. Here is a young man who managed to defeat defenses that have held for two hundred years! Surely he carries the DNA that reflects intelligence and persistence. Are these not the very characteristics that you want to introduce into our community?"

Peter stood to speak. "Fear not, little sister! We do not need to keep him alive for that. Our sperm banks will store his DNA for you quite satisfactorily.' Peter grinned at his sister. 'That way he does not have to dishonor you again by putting his disgusting body against yours!"

Pocahontas deliberately ran her eyes over me. Her gaze swept me from head to toe. This time I felt embarrassed. I don't think, however, that she was displeased with what she saw. Only when she was finished did she turn angrily toward her brother, though she spoke to her father and the Council of Elders.

"Father, I wish to claim this boy as my future mate. Under our laws, I have the right to choose my mate. I choose him!"

Her brother was furious, and the faces of most of the Elders expressed shock. Peter replied in an enraged tone.

"You dare to choose an outsider!? This has not happened for two hundred years! And you choose one who has dishonored our family!"

"You still haven't told me what you were doing in the bushes, brother-of-mine! How dare you accuse this man of a crime that you yourself commit? I am much more ashamed that you would spy on your own sister. And I wonder how Turtle Dove's family will feel when they find out that you did the same to her!"

Peter turned and ran from the room. His moment of glory was over, and he was probably in serious trouble with both his own family and that of Turtle Dove's. And if that was upsetting, I could just imagine how he felt about his soon-to-be brother-in-law! I smiled. I couldn't wait to get a ride in one of the jump-jets.

**If this story seems familiar, that is
because it is a variation on the
brainwashing theme I used first in
Janissary. This story appeared in the
November 2002 edition of THIS WAY
UP.**

8. PRISONS OF YOUR MIND

I wake quickly, eager to get to work again. The
chow-line is moving, so I join the slowly snaking line of
men. It's gruel again; my favorite. I stand close to the guy
in front of me, but he don't say nothing, and neither do I.
Most of us just want to get to the quarry. I bolt my chow,
and am left with a few minutes of time before I am
allowed to start work.

I make my bed and wash my face and hands.
Cleanliness is next to Godliness, or so John tells me. I am
excited when the work whistle finally blows. The two
suns are finally in a low line, parallel with the horizon. I
sigh with relief. It's the signal for the working day to
begin.

I hurry through the purple grass, toward the quarry. I
can hardly wait to get there. I feel sure that this week I
will set a personal record for the most ore dug.

As I move over the grass and into the shelter of the
brown-leaved trees, I have another attack of deja vu. I am
somewhere else, and the trees are an impossible shade of
green. Instead of an orange sky, I see a blue one! I shake

my head, trying to physically dislodge my waking dream. I hurry, hoping that I can leave the disturbing vision behind.

Eagerly I swing my pick. Enthusiastically I scoop the ore up with my shovel, and throw it into my wheelbarrow.

I keep admiring the wheelbarrow as I work. It is almost new, and the bright red paint on it still gleams. It had been given me in recognition of my efforts the previous month. John, our supervisor, had presented it to me in front of all the assembled men.

I was so proud! I had felt the waves of envy sweep through the ranks. I do know that I have to work even harder to be designated 'worker of the month' two times in a row. There are many who envy me my good fortune, and they are pushing themselves into exhaustion in order to try and surpass my record. I'm not ready to give up without a fight, however.

My pick takes on a life of its own, hurling itself against the hard rock again and again. The blisters on my right hand break, but I don't feel any pain.

In spite of my efforts to sublimate all my energies into my work, another errant vision attaches itself to me, and insists on playing out its script. Three government thugs have found us and seized a little girl. A woman is on the ground. She screams and screams, until my head aches from the noise. Marisa. Suddenly I know the name of the little girl. She is our third, and our genetic license only allows for two children!

The implement in my hands does not attack the vegetable garden, but instead leaps unbidden at the hulking government goons. They part before me, and they dance backwards. My body knows panic. The fate of an illegal child is unequivocal. They are not going to kill my little girl!

The men have not obeyed my command to let my daughter go. I strike again and again at the three goons.

They are agile, but I finally connect, and one falls to the ground. I attack the second, but the third circles behind me. I feel hands grabbing me . . . I turn in great fear, to see John standing there.

"Buddy, are you OK? Did you have another dream?"

My body has not recovered from the shock of all the bio-enzymes that have so recently flooded my system. Yet I play it cagey. I know that if I tell John the truth, I might not be allowed to work tomorrow. Sent to sick-bay, I would be forced to sit in idleness. Last month, Pete, one of the few men I had liked enough to chat with, had had a lot of visions. He had reported them to John. First John had him rest for a few days, and then some strangers came and took him away.

Another man named Pedro joined us a few days later, to replace Pete. He looked just like Pete, so I went up to him to shoot-the-breeze, but he didn't know me, and he had a very different personality. I didn't like Pedro at all.

"Thanks, I'm fine. I think I just pushed myself a little too hard! You know I want to be worthy of my beautiful wheelbarrow."

John smiles at me. "Well, you just take it easy! You know you're one of the finest workers I ever had. And if you do have any strange dreams, you just let me know. The doctors can cure them, you know."

"No . . . no, it's nothing like that. I'll just take a little break for water, and then get right back to work."

"O.K., old timer! You just take as long a break as you need. You're doin' great this month. You don't have to work yourself to death!"

"Thanks John. I'll be real careful."

I walk slowly to the water barrel. I can feel John's eyes following me as I take the ladle and dip it into the sweet water. I think about what John said. It seems funny. He calls me 'old-timer', but I think I am actually younger than him. Under his hat his hair is sparse, and what there is, is gray.

The rippled reflection in the water barrel shows me a weathered face, but the hair, when it is not shaved, is black. I know John is concerned about me, and I promise myself I will work even harder for him tomorrow. Perhaps, if I show I am up to it, he will let me do some overtime.

The twin suns are both setting as I walk the long walk back to camp. I squint a little, and there suddenly seems to be one too many suns in the sky! Again I have a feeling the sky should be going gold or red, not muddy brown. John told me that these twin suns have been setting just so for over two billion years, so I wonder how I could imagine it otherwise. Two suns are natural! A single sun would not be right. I cannot imagine how I dreamed of such a thing.

I must not let these dreams escape from my unconscious mind! They have to be banished to the world of sleep. My head aches, my feet drag, and John catches up with me and catches my arm.

"What's wrong, old-timer?"

My mouth opens to deny any problems, but suddenly I see before me a stranger who has laid hands on me. He seems to be trying to arrest me. I only know something terrible will happen if I let him! This man is the law! I strike out at him with all the force of my right arm. Even as the man/John crumples, I spin and begin to run a zig-zag pattern toward the woods.

The trees look like mis-colored abominations from a nursery-school wall, but I am too busy to wonder about this new incongruity. I know somehow that more than my life depends upon me reaching those woods before the minions of the law reach me.

Three burley security types in white lab coats head after me. Each of the three of them could be mistaken for walking tree trunks, but I don't have time to admire their physiques. For all their bulk, these guys can run like the wind!

"Earth!" The word pops unbidden into my head. Is that where I come from? Did I once live there? What the hell is the Tau Beta Penal Colony? I visualize a yellow sun and a blue sky again, superimposed on a little girl's terrified face. Suddenly I don't have time to think about these strange thoughts. The three goons have reached me.

I spin, and my foot lashes out at the first one. To my surprise, he goes down. I trade a few punches with the second one, but the third circles behind me. My peripheral vision picks up a rapidly-moving branch the thickness of my wrist! It connects with my head, and I feel my consciousness fading. In the final moment before I collapse, the memories of my family, and the struggle, finally floods clearly into my mind.

My name is Douglas, and Dr. Peterson tells me I was born on this beautiful planet just this morning. Dr. Peterson tells me I couldn't possibly remember my birth, but I do. I vaguely remember an angel in white removing little wires from my head, and then Dr. Peterson himself unstrapped all these thick straps that held me to my birth chair. He helps me out of the chair, and tells me to hustle. He says he has to help two more 'births' before he can go home today.

Dr. Peterson hands me a bundle of stuff he calls clothing. I have never worn any before, but I seem to automatically know what to do with them. I shrug them on. Dr. Peterson urges me again to hurry. He says my new supervisor, a guy named John, is waiting outside for me. John is apparently going to teach me the rudiments of quarrying ore from an open-pit mine. It sounds like an exciting and responsible job. I can hardly wait to get started.

I have to give credit to the story, War of
the Worlds, by H. G Wells, for the
inspiration of this story. I did enjoy
taking the story in other directions,
however. My story first appeared in the
September 2001 edition of
ALTERNATE REALITIES.

9. Fe2O3

The great silver shape hurtled through the void.
When it reached the upper ionosphere, it traced out a path
of blazing light. A young couple, nestled together on a
nameless beach in Egypt saw its glowing flare. They
wished on it. In Diego Garcia the great antennae paused
in their questing. Powerful tracking computers focused on
the unknown object.

An emergency telephone jumped in London. "No,
Military Intelligence knows nothing of a rocket over
Africa."

Washington's response was the same. "No. The
NASA computers don't list one single damn piece of
space junk that has an ETA within the next two weeks.
Call the observatory and see if we're scheduled to get any
meteorite showers. Yah? Same to you."

In spite of Perestroika, alarms rang and nuclear subs
slipped from their docks in both the Russian Federation
and North America. The rest of the world slept. The
unidentified object blew a hundred foot crater in the

parched earth of the African veld. Oddly, its physical characteristics were not changed in any way.

When dawn painted the African veldt crimson, the same decision had been reached in both London and Washington. The UFO could have been an untracked piece of the 'space junk', orbited by the Russians or Americans, or for that matter, the French or Japanese. Alternatively, it could conceivably have been a large meteorite. Or, it really could be something totally unknown. The alert made the third page of several world dailies. In London, the Times didn't even mention it.

A slight tremor in Bwanda had been recorded by several seismological centers. Two American military satellites were quietly re-tasked and assigned the job of finding the landing site. The possibility that the object could have been an unknown Russian satellite made the Americans curious. If it was manmade, then the object had to be located and examined.

As the dawn broke, Jemo's mother shook his naked right shoulder. "Wake now, my sweet son, and go find the herd. It will soon be time for milking."

Jemo crawled sleepily from under his blanket. With amazing rapidity, the sun leap-frogged the horizon. Before Jemo had finished his sketchy toilet and snatched a hunk of cheese, the land was bathed in brilliant sunshine.

The boy whistled to his dog and set off at a steady jog to find the family's cattle. Already he could feel the parched earth reflecting the harsh radiance of the sun. He dreamed of the monsoon season, when the veld burst into a verdant paradise. The scorched earth, now cracked and almost lifeless, would again support lush grass. His family's cattle, now lean and hungry, would fill out, and, even better, would no longer need to be allowed to wander each night.

In spite of the danger from the occasional roving

predators from one of the nature preserves, he knew it was necessary in the dry season if the cattle were to survive. Already they were gaunt. His family had to live on a meager harvest of milk. Within weeks, days, however, the cows would be sleek again, and generous with their milk.

As Jemo ran towards the hollow where his charges generally spent their nights, he noticed strange flashes of light, almost as if reflecting off metal. But who would have metal in his father's pastures? Besides, the amount of reflected light seemed to indicate much too large a structure for anyone to set up overnight.

Jemo noticed his dog hesitate. For the boy, brought up where life depended on animal senses, that was a bad sign. He crossed himself, as he had once seen priests doing in an outdoor church service. The white men had mostly gone from his peoples' lands, but he knew that they had had powerful magic.

He approached the shiny object cautiously. His every sense was alert and questing. He climbed out of the slight ravine which was his accustomed path. Jemo froze; uncomprehending. Before him was a vast metallic globe. Surrounding it was a series of smaller domes.

Even as he climbed out of the ravine, a long slim turret swung in his direction. It paused, and then a jet of pure light struck both the boy and his canine companion. The air was filled with a sickeningly-sweet odor, and a few scraps of charred flesh littered the ground.

The game warden rode slowly. After an all-night attempt to track the elephant poachers who had hit the game preserve to the west, both he and his horse were exhausted.

As he mounted the last major hill before the local chief's village, something caught his eye. The sun's rays were bouncing off something huge and metallic. He clucked to his faithful horse and moved down to investigate. Suddenly he noticed a metal humanoid which had some kind of tube pointed right at him.

He pulled his horse up immediately. It was too late. The headless body of the game warden's horse toppled forward.

Even as he fell, the man grabbed his .500 Magnum express rifle. His nostrils churned at the stench of the burned horse flash. From behind the headless horse, he took careful aim and pulled both triggers, one after the other.

The two hammers struck and two huge slugs, each one with over twenty-five tons of kinetic energy behind it, struck the dazzling robot-like creature in the head. The metal creature paused for a moment, and digested the implications of this new attack. Then a second jet of light lanced out. Even the warden's gun-barrel melted.

Colonel Jomolo and his two bush-boys careened over the top of the hillock. The Colonel was a frustrated race driver, and his little flat-head four cylinder was a poor excuse for a racing machine. He was worried, however. His best game warden was several hours late in reporting in. Hunting poachers was a deadly game, and the man should have been back long before.

Immediately they topped the rise, the three of them noticed the long shiny fence. It enclosed several acres of land. The Colonel slammed on the brakes, and the Jeep slid to a quivering halt.

It was the last thing Colonel Jomolo was to do. One of his boys, with a more acute sense of danger, or just more luck, jumped out of the vehicle. He threw himself to the ground and stared as the Jeep and its occupants reached a liquid, and then a gaseous stage. He crawled back over the top of the hill and then ran as fast as his sturdy legs would carry him.

President Kayitesi, President-for-Life of Bwanda, was a courageous man. Hearing of the mysterious threat for the first time, he immediately hurled his entire air force, comprised of seven Hawker-Hurricanes, at the alien structure. After his air force reported a hundred percent loss of its craft, he hurled curses, both obscene and superstitious. Finally, after his curses and his Commander-in-Chief's western science didn't work, he admitted defeat.

He decided to call both the U.S. and Russia. He missed the good old days when they competed for his attention so assiduously. Still, it was always fun to see who would offer the most.

"Yes, President Gore, I know I had to do something. In the interests of western democracy and our friendship with your great country, I sent my entire fleet of jet fighters against the enemy. Not one of my heroic pilots came back, Mr. President! Not one!

You said to send some good men in. Well, I did! I sent my entire Personal Guard. They are all dead! Do you know what that means, Mr. Gore? If the Butu scoundrels who make up the majority of the population find out, they might rebel against both their lawful government and their illustrious leader.

How am I going to reason with them if I have no Personal Guard or air force? You know, Mr. Gore, strafing runs are such a GREAT incentive to peace. You do not use them against your domestic enemies?"

"No? And you have so many beautiful planes. What a pity. Mr. President, I did my best to keep the world safe for democracy, and my effort, valiant as it was, might yet cost me my life! Sir, I am going to need a great deal of military aid to replace my losses, and I am going to need it immediately."

"What am I thinking of? How about a squadron or two of those F16s? And of course I will need ground crews and munitions. Oh, and perhaps the CIA can arrange for some pilots until you are able to train me new ones. They must have some lying around. "

"Mr. President, my dear friend, I can only be of help to you if I hold the reins of power here securely, and I would much rather have your fine aircraft than worn out Migs."

"Yes, of course I will let in American advisors. We will even let them use American dollars to buy whatever goods they need. I will make sure that they are put up in style, and I will personally ensure that they are not gouged on the rent."

"No, you do need to thank me. it is the least I can do for our American friends. When do you think the first of my F16s will arrive?"

General Robertson, commander of the American Fast Deployment Force, stared through the massive telescope at the lines of silver men. The enemy creatures stood perfectly still, while, nearby, other machines excavated earth. Yet others trundled the soil to vast domes, from which exited yet more metal men.

"Well, Colonel, you have been studying the metal-heads for over a week, now. What the hell am I watching?"

"We can't be sure, sir, but as near as we can ascertain, it looks as if they are mining for ore."

"So they are building their damned robots from our soil?"

"It sure looks that way, General."

"Then every day counts! A few weeks ago, they had regiments of their metal men. Now they have divisions! Napoleon said it. 'Strength lies not in defense, but in attack!'"

"Ah, I think that was Hitler, sir."

"Do I look like a man who would quote Hitler, Colonel?"

"No, sir!"

"Then it was obviously Napoleon who said it. Now, I

want you to plan an attack in force."

"Sir, Bwanda's Personal Guard went in less than two weeks ago. Not one of them returned."

"The prime minister's-for-life Personal Guard! Most of them are probably still running!"

"Sir, many of them were trained by the British SAS. They were good."

"Well, then, now they're dead! I concede, Colonel, that they might have been good riflemen. We will fully apply modern industry to the art of war. You, sir, will use heavy armor, gun ships, and arrange massive artillery support. I want a full-scale blitzkrieg, and, yes, I know that was Hitler's battle tactic.

Don't spare the expenses, Colonel. Bring in whatever you need. The entire air force is at your disposal . . . If you have no further questions, sir, I suggest that you get moving!"

"Well, Colonel, how're we doing?"

"I regret to report, General, that the American 34th Armored Division is gone."

"Of course it's gone. They were to move up over an hour ago!"

"No, sir. They're gone - dead. There are none of them left, General, sir!"

"What the fuck are you talking about, son?!"

"They attacked as ordered, sir. As far as we know, they're wiped out."

"Son, you're saying NONE survived?"

"A few tanks put up a smoke screen and managed to break off contact. The enemy weapons don't work well in heavy smoke."

"And the rest?"

"As for the rest - there is no rest."

The general sighed. "Well, it's a hell of a price to pay, but at least we found a weakness."

"Yes, sir, that's the good news."

"You have MORE bad new, Colonel?"

"Yes, sir. The metal men came after us. They have broken through their own perimeter, and are destroying everything they come across. Several villages have already gone up in flame, and they are moving fast!"

"Yes, Mr. Gore. It is good to hear your voice, too. No, I am not in Moscow. I am enjoying a little time at my dacha. It is very peaceful here."

"President Gore, let me get this straight. You wish to launch a nuclear-tipped intercontinental ballistic missile against the - what you call metal-heads? Do you really think that there is no other solution?"

"Yes, I know that my Spetsnaz did no better than your 34th Armored . . . The British lost HOW many SAS?"

The Russian president sighed. "I understand your wish to use such a weapon. Should the winds blow northwards, however, there is a great risk of radioactive fallout over my country. My people have suffered greatly after Chernobyl. They would not be happy to hear that the radioactivity is coming again."

"Yes, our mass shelters still exist. To move all our people to our shelters would shut down industry and cost a great deal of money; however, money which you must appreciate, we do not currently have in our treasury."

"Yes? Well if you are willing to take care of all the costs, then I guess I cannot argue. I suppose that we have to take bold steps."

The long-range artillery and rocket barrage lifted. A thousand miles to the west, a submarine Captain and his Chief Executive Officer simultaneously turned their special keys and pushed the 'fire' button. In a great spurt of seawater, the nuclear-tipped missile took to the air.

The elaborate guidance system guided the missile unerringly. The rocket came down well within the alien perimeter. There was a thunderous explosion, and a thick mushroom cloud leapt into the clear blue sky.

General Robertson sat in his radiation-proof command vehicle and waited for word of the results. "You just wait and see, Colonel, this will take care of your little metal men. Did you know that the temperature in the middle of that fireball actually surpassed that of the sun's surface? No substance known to man can survive such temperatures."

"Sir, the fallout is heading for several major cities.

"Son, we knew that there would be some collateral damage. That was the price we had to pay to stop this invasion!"

"General, the Russkis were in shelters, and the wind is unlikely to even take the radiation there."

"Yes, well, Colonel, we had to do something to pacify them. Otherwise they were going to refuse to let us use a Big One. Even as it was, they went to Defcon 2."

The major manning the Satcom system turned to his two superior officers. "Sirs, we are getting a message from Washington . . . Satellite surveillance reports that the metal man just launched an offensive against Nairobi . . . Sir! The first photos show no damage to the main domes!"

The Colonel couldn't keep his look of satisfaction off his face. "Well, General. After poisoning millions of our own people, we seem to have done little more than piss the metal-heads off."

"Lose the smirk, Colonel. It'll be your wife and children those metal monsters will be coming for! . . . Not now, Major! Can't you that I'm busy?"

"It's the president, sir."

"Tell that pinhead to get stuffed! His damned planes are on the way, and if he tries to hold us up for anything else, tell him I am considering a very generous Butu offer."

"Not that President, General."

"President Gore? Why didn't you say so, you moron!"

"Yes, Mr. President. It looked like a direct hit. We won't be able to send anybody forward to check for another day or two, however, even with radiation shielding, sir."

"Really? Both Nairobi and Addis Ababa? Well sir, Nairobi isn't a big loss, anyway. The latest report I had is that it's still glowing with radiation. It really does sound like we stirred them up, however!"

"No, sir. I'm not surprised that the United Nations World Military Command is upset. I know we promised that the Big One would end the menace. I guess we were wrong."

"Sir, that's very nice, but the President-for-Life's advisors tell me that the monsoons are only days away. Indications are that the rain will mean the grounding of most of the surveillance craft. It'll also produce a major logistical problem for the various forces the U.N. has put on the ground here. Most of the roads will become impassible."

"No, sir, it won't be weeks. I'm told the rain will pose major problems for months."

A despondent world waited for the steady rains to slacken so the newly formed United Nations World Military Command could stubbornly take on the seemingly invulnerable alien enemy yet again. They had run out of ideas, but it was not in their nature to give up.

"Yes, Mr. President. It's General McCarthy here again. Yes, sir, I am wearing my blue hat. Thank you for arranging to make me commander-in-chief of the U.N. forces."

"Yes, sir, I am sure that you had to call in a lot of favors, after our little problems. But we're ready again just as soon as the rain lets up. "

"Well, we have a hundred thousand Chinese

volunteer troops ready to go, just as soon as the roads are dry enough that they can walk in."

"Radiation? Well, we have suited them up as best we can. They are volunteer soldiers, Mr. President. They know the risks."

"Good news, Mr. President! The Third Volunteer Shanghai Suicide squad has crossed the enemy lines, and returned."

"No, it's a first, sir! No one else has ever made it back."

"What did they find, sir? That's what's so interesting. They found the first line of metal-heads just waiting for them. The plan was for the volunteers to get as close as they could and then set off the satchel charges they had strapped to their stomachs."

"Sure it would be hard on them, sir. That's why they're volunteers. Anyway, the preliminary report is that the metal-heads, standing in their thousands, just let the troops walk right up to them."

"Why? That's the interesting part, Mr. President. They said that all the little metal-heads were conscious. They just couldn't move. Unbelievable as it may sound, the answer just seemed to be good ol' Fe_2O_3."

"What, sir? No, sir, I'm not trying to be funny."

"Yes, sir! I am trying to tell you what happened! It's rust, sir! The metalheads are all rusted solid!"

The next three stories tell the adventures of a human officer who finds love and a new destiny with an alien princess. Freed of his military brainwashing, he joins the Vuorrans, an alien race targeted for annihilation by an evil Terran emperor. He soon finds himself commander of a rag-tag force of civilians, fighting the greatest empire in the galaxy. How can a small band of rebels take on the galaxy's greatest military power and win? That was the challenge I set myself.

Eventually these short stories became chapters, and the whole eventually transmogrified into a Science Fiction novel, THE VUORRAN POGROM.

10. THE GAME BEGINS.

The thirteen ships comprising our little fleet broke out of Hyperspace at precisely the same moment. Such formation flying was never attempted by civilian vessels, but I had seen it done so often by the Dominion navy that I knew there was little real danger to it. Space Station Theta 42 was dead ahead. In the midst of our little Vuorran fleet was one of the kilometer-long particle-beam projectors, recently rebuilt as a star ship!

As smoothly as we had practiced a hundred times, the

various trader ships slipped closer to their pre-assigned positions; until they were able to couple with the framework of power leads awaiting them. Alone, even the multiple fusion-generators that the Vuorrans had cobbled together and put within the long projector-hull were simply not powerful enough to bring the giant weapon up to anything approaching full power. With all thirteen ships in the power harness, however, it was a very different situation. We now had a weapon that was more powerful than anything aboard the greatest Terran Dreadnought.

The Vuorran weapon was, by the nature of its size, a bugger to manoeuver, and it was completely unarmored. As I had explained to the Vuorran High Command, however, we were facing a commercial space station, not a Dominion battle fleet.

The information garnered by Richard Kent and our non-human scouts seemed to be dead on. Our long-range vision scanners confirmed what our multi-sensor radars had already told us; there was only one military vessel, in a tight orbit by the space station. All the other vessels' transponders registered as commercial freighters.

I grinned at Cattrina, my very own Vuorran princess. "O ye of little faith! Look, my princess. It is as we had hoped."

Within thirty seconds after breaking through the six-dimensional wall, our ships had all moved to their assigned position.

"Well, 'Tinhead'?' I spoke to the 'puter of our little flagship, the once and former Terran naval vessel I had escaped in from Croton III. 'Are all the ships locked into the grid yet and fired up?"

"Yes, Centurion."

The giant weapon was ready!

"Princess, you may say the word."

Cattrina grinned at me. "If you think that you are

going to shift all the blame for this little expedition, then you are dreaming!"

"Actually, I think the Emperor is already a little pissed off at me, but he's going to be really happy if we let that ship escape!"

We both looked at each other and counted down together. "Three. Two. One. Fire!"

We were condemning good men to death, but at last the Vuorrans were finally striking back. Millions of their citizens, men, women, and children, were lying dead on countless planets. Their home world was interdicted, and any battered survivors of the pogrom had been brutally enslaved, all by order of the Terran High Command and the evil emperor. Only one little band of rebels remained free, and I was proud to be a part of them. In fact, not to brag, but they had appointed me, a Terran, as their supreme military commander!

I knew just how brutally the pogrom was being instituted, because in my fairly recent past I had been a Centurion in the Imperial forces. Only the love of Cattrina, and her incredible mind, had rescued me from being a part of the horror the Emperor had ordered.

On our signal, Tinhead sent the electronic signal to all ships in the grid. The giant tube seemed to hum. The business end of the tube glowed, and a second later portions of the Dominion Frigate glowed white hot. The crew had not had time to power-up their shields, and in truth it would have mattered little. The power of the beam was incredible. The frigate became incandescent, and then just seemed to fade away. I spoke again to Tinhead.

"Cease fire! Keep the particle beam on 'orange alert' in case we have to fire quickly. Switch on the comm and prepare to broadcast on all commercial wavelengths. Cut in the audio on my command . . . Now! Attention Space station Theta 42! This is the Free Vuorran Navy! Any ships who attempt to get underway will meet the same fate as the late Dominion frigate!

All shields are to be lowered immediately. Refusal to comply will be construed as a hostile act and will be punished without any further warnings! All vessels will stand by for boardings of armed Vuorran personnel. 'Puter, cut signal!"

I turned away from the mike and breathed a sigh of relief. My hand stretched out until I could touch the arm of a royal princess. All I could do now was to hope that the next phase went well. I prayed that the Dominion ship captains didn't realize that our single weapon, powerful as it was, was so unwieldy that they could probably make their distance to null grav before we could bring the giant tube to bear.

The tube was singularly vulnerable to hostile fire, but of course that is why we had felt obligated to take out the frigate without warning. I was sorry that brave Terran marines and sailors had had to die so precipitously, but a single effective warship would easily have destroyed our huge and unwieldy weapon.

I knew too, from my own previous life, that the naval personnel would not have been able to surrender to us if they had wanted to. Their rigid conditioning would have ensured that they died to the last man.

The three designated troop-carriers slipped out of their position in the power-net, and eased their way towards the twenty-odd freighters that hung in space tight against the space station. When they neared the ships a swarm of tiny dots in the holographic box indicated that my Vuorran marines had launched.

I stood in my excitement. "There they go, my love! If we pull this off, it just could paralyze the Empire's trade."

My eyes remained glued to the holographic box. A Vuorran squad per enemy ship, the tiny dots spread out towards the various freighters. Now was the time of greatest risk! If the crews chose to fight, they could probably easily hold-off the Vuorran troopers, though I knew that the Vuorran marines were very, very, good.

I ought to know! I had trained them, yelled at them, and bullied them, until they were, with their unhuman super-quick reflexes, a match for the best Dominion marines I had ever seen or led. Their military equipment, however, was minimal. Only one in four Vuorran marines were encased in the old Terran space-armor that had been stored on my 'flagship'; the little naval vessel I had purloined from Croton III. The rest of the marines wore only regular commercial-issue space suits. No one on the other side should have known that, however, and I wasn't about to tell them!

Suddenly my musings were interrupted by the ship computer. "Attention! Attention, Major Bruce! Freighter now marked as green on my holographic projection has started its drive engines! Instructions please!"

I knew that the power-grid was unavoidably short power after we pulled the three 'troop-carriers' out of it. We were short ships. This raid had, in fact, been intended to resolve exactly that problem. Our calculations had said that ten ships might be able to supply enough power for the particle beam. It was time to find out!

"Tinhead, warn all ships in the net that they will need a ten percent generator overload at your signal! Instruct all launched marines in the vicinity of the target ship to hit their rocket-pods hard and evacuate! Order all shields down and ships on minimal power draw! Fire when the capacitors reach minimal necessary power and the marines are clear. Commence now!"

I sat back and watched the holographic box fearfully. If the vessel got moving before we were ready, we could never bring our cumbersome weapon to bear in time. And if we did, the others could easily slip away while we were desperately maneuvering the giant tube back.

The ship had just started to ease away from the

station, however, when the particle beam capacitors reached their minimal acceptable energy level. The ships in the circuit had managed to stay attached as the huge vessel shifted its bulk slightly. The tiny dots that represented the marines were well away.

I watched the brilliant beam shoot out on the holographic projection, and the freighter too, suddenly just seemed to disappear. The only hint of its previous existence was the plethora of tiny bits of flotsam rapidly vacating the area of the ships' demise.

It was obvious that our message was clear, for no other ship attempted the same trick. Our prize-crews rocketed back and one by one boarded the twenty-odd vessels. One by one they reported that the former occupants had departed for the space station, and that the ships were now Free Vuorran naval vessels!

As the new and old Vuorran vessels manoeuvred into formation and then fled into hyperspace, I knew that we had just thrown the gauntlet in the Emperor's face. The game had begun!

This is the second short story in the Vuorran series. How could a small rebel force land on a heavily protected planet and rescue hundreds of thousands of Vuorran captives? That was the challenge.

11. THE ROYAL PRINCESS.

We walked towards the dawn. The sky ahead of us lightened further, and then silently burst into crimson. Once the crimson peaked, the colors started a slight shift towards the blue end of the spectrum that was the daylight norm on Atrium.

The column marched single file, though we had flankers out in front and on the sides so that we would not walk into any unpleasant surprises. My little band of rebels had many kilometers to cover before we dared let the Terran authorities know that we were on-planet. Discovery at this point would inevitably mean death. We'd let the Terrans know we were on the planet soon enough. We just wanted to control the timing. Timing was everything!

I called a break at noon. "Alright, you guys! Get a couple of hours of sleep. You deserve it."

As the men spread out in the shade, I leaned against a tree. I would nap standing up, a little trick I had learned when I was still a young soldier in the Terran Marines.

We had decided to travel largely by day. The infrared scanners so favored by the Terran military would be much more likely to pick up the heat radiating from our bodies at night. The sunlight meant that there was a greater temperature variance by day than night.

Of course, the reciprocal corollary of this was that we would be much more noticeable to any aerial scanners that relied on color-vision. We had long debated the alternatives, and had even run experiments on the surface of Haven II, the new planet that the Vuorran scouts had discovered a few months earlier and was in the direction of . . . I honestly didn't know.

The Vuorran scientists had carefully located and dissolved my brain's protein lattice that had held that specific memory. There was no way that any of us could, if caught alive, betray the location of the Vuorran last refuge. What we DID know was a galactic co-ordinate that would bring us back to the vicinity of a Vuorran scout ship. Only after convincing the commander of the scout ship of our identity would we be allowed to advance to Galactic Position Two, where another scout would ensure that we were not being followed before giving us the location of Galactic Position Three. From there we could travel directly to Haven II.

In any event, our trials had determined that travel by day was as safe as by night, as long as the Terrans didn't have remote surveillance equipment out specifically looking for us. We had to assume that this was unlikely. After all, the Vuorran captives were held on another island continent, and there was no dangerous indigenous wildlife. Besides, no Vuorrans in their right minds would attempt to land on a planet from which they had no escape. No vessel could ever hope to clear the atmosphere without permission of the Terran High Command. I had done it once, but I had cleared atmosphere in a naval ship with its transponder transmitting the appropriate coded signal; from a planet that was not expecting anything untoward from its own naval base. The resulting confusion had allowed me to make it, but even that had been a close thing, and the odds of pulling it off in an unknown craft, on a planet where the authorities were trigger-happy, was infinitesimal.

Besides, to pull it off, we needed a vessel capable of rapid acceleration and hyperspace travel. Our modified escape pod didn't even carry enough fuel to allow us to break free from the planet's gravity well.

After a several hour rest, we ate a cold meal, buried the evidence of our presence, and moved out. I had all the patrol put on their masking cloaks, but we did not turn on the fields since experience showed that it was difficult for us to travel far that way. Though we could order our helmet vision systems to switch to the wave band which detected the telltale field pattern, it was inconvenient for walking in daylight. Further, I hesitated to use our very finite electrical power at this point. I feared that we would need it later as we approached the Terran settlement.

Thus we walked boldly forward, susceptible to aerial spy-eyes. We had to take risks somewhere, however, and this one was a calculated one. Besides, we had their secret weapon with us. Cattrina, small and delicate as she appeared, was capable of both sensing the presence and feelings of others from a distance. She also had just finished exhaustive training in mental manipulation of electronic brains. In a laboratory setting, she had shown an incredible ability to control a 'puter, just by sensing its electro-magnetic field and merging her own with it. I knew that she was not capable of reading a computer's 'thoughts', just as she had not been able to read my thoughts when we had first met, yet I well remembered how she placed her hands on my brow and took some of my terrible pain unto herself. She told me afterwards that she had been able to sense my aura, and could 'see' the twist in it. By attempting to 'smooth' the twist out, she had found herself able to change the shape and color of my aura, until it was once again 'smooth' and uniform in color.

Somehow, perhaps without realizing it, she had been able to permanently erase the Emperor's imprinting. Aboard ship on the way to the planet I now thought of as Haven I, she had put her hands on the 'puter, and managed to do the same. These were the very skills she had been working hard to hone. We were counting on these incredible skills. In fact, the fate of the entire mission was predicated on her successfully using this ability against the Terran 'puters.

By turning on the anti-grav belts to their lowest setting, we were able to effectively cut the weight of our bodies so that we weighed only a portion of our usual weight. We had each found through practice the ideal minimal weight; light enough that we could trot all day without serious body strain, but heavy enough that we did not float helplessly into the air at each careless step.

When dusk came we prepared for the night. The cool of the evening would make us stand out like flares to aerial spy-eyes. We sought shelter under large trees. If necessary, we would switch on our masking cloaks and breathe self-contained air. That would hide us from carbon-dioxide, visual, and infra-red scanners. But again, our fuel-packs were finite, and we had to risk something now so we would be able to use our high-tech equipment later; when we approached the settlements and the risk of discovery grew.

The group reviewed the plan for the last time. Each man was finally able to repeat it verbatim, and I had even ported the precise plans to each man's mini-'puter as a final backup.

Cattrina stood watching me play the role of

Centurion with my Vuorran troops. As they moved off to try and get closer to their assigned positions before zero hour, I took a minute for my private life. Major Bruce, acting in the capacity as Centurion, had done his job with what he felt was professionalism. HISTAKH Timm wanted a moment with his loved one before going into battle!

I did not need Cattrina's psychic skills to read her feelings. Her eyes, gigantic by Human standards, seemed oddly watery. Her heart was hammering in her chest. I did not comment verbally, but instead just hugged her tight, until she could hardly breathe. For a few moments it didn't matter, as my lips were pressed hard against hers.

We clung to each other as if there might be no tomorrow. If anything went wrong in our plan, there WOULD be no tomorrow, at least for us. After an all too brief few moments, I let go, attempted to memorize her face with one last look, and then turned to follow my troopers. As I strode after the men, I could feel her warmth and love wash over and through me, easing slightly the solid lump that was my stomach.

The troopers had all in turn switched on their masking cloaks, and I was forced to order my vision system to switch to the wave band that allowed me to clearly see my own men. Once our little group reached what I had determined to be close to the Terran security perimeter, I ordered the Vuorrans forward on their bellies. Two Vuorrans I kept back, however, to stay behind and guard the Princess.

She was the secret of this mission. Without her we could not succeed, and now was not the battle we had brought her for. I knew she was annoyed at me for holding her back and assigning her bodyguards, but she understood the hierarchy of command, and did not argue with me. Besides, she did not have a masking cloak to use. During our journey there, I had shared mine with her.

The cloaks were secret Terran military items, and no amount of bribes in the Free Zones had been enough to spring any loose. Since money could buy anything there, I had had to assume that there were simply no contraband ones to be had. Instead, we had left Vuorran scientists on Haven II with schematics of the ones that came with my stolen Squad transport. In time the Vuorrans would be able to duplicate them, but for now we had to make do with the purloined twenty-five.

I saw the five units split up and head for their pre-assigned positions around the military headquarters. I had read once of a long-ago war on Terra where commandos had slipped silently into one of the barracks and slit the throat of every other sleeping soldier. The survivors had been so rattled that they surrendered soon after, although they in fact greatly outnumbered the attackers. I would have liked to try it! The Vuorrans were easily capable of it, except for the many electronic sentry systems normally scattered around Terran headquarters buildings.

Cattrina had felt that she might be able to manage the varied sensor 'puters, but I feared that something might go wrong. She had, in fact, shown incredible skill in "massaging" the 'puter units we had at the Institute for Computer Research on Haven II. I knew it would only take one computer system to betray us, however. One error before we were ready, and we all died! I had asked her to try and control the master 'puter, but only after we had made our move.

I looked through my vision-enhancers at the base ahead. The Terran troops who we could see marching and counter-marching around the drill square looked to be second rate soldiers; 'groundhoppers' in the Terran Marine slang. They were, after all, probably locals shanghaied to guard helpless prisoners.

There was a modest naval task force in the sky to protect against just such as us, but we had calculated that the Terrans would not take the idea of a ground attack too seriously. Their main task was presumably to keep the Vuorran prisoners at work until they died, or their fate was otherwise decreed.

I whispered the word into my battle comm. The scrambled word leapt at the speed of light to all twenty-three troopers scattered around the buildings and parade square. As quickly de-scrambled and fed into their subcutaneous receivers, it galvanized the troopers into action.

Squads one and two, the two mech squads, were securely hidden in a gully to my left. Before stealthily advancing to join the upcoming battle, they loosed their flocks of anti-personnel Sky Hunters into the air. The small devices, shaped and sized much like ancient oversized (and extinct) Terran bees, hovered, and then headed slowly in the direction that the Vuorran team had programmed them to head in, quite as if they were truly bees, and the Vuorran software had done a little dance in the hive in order to orient them to the direction of the flowers. In truth, the Vuorrans had, and the Sky Hunters headed out faithfully in search for their 'flowers'. They were programmed for considerable delay before seeking targets. I wanted them to hang around awhile before getting serious. First I wanted my team to chase up a few targets!

Squads three and four, widely dispersed, aimed their anti-personnel rifles (APR's) at the perimeter guards and any visible officers. Long ago I had been taught that the soldiers were the tentacles of the giant creature that is an army. If you cut off one tentacle, another would take its place. By killing the officers, however, you cut out the brains. The separate tentacles wither without the cohesion brought by the officers. Thus, the officers were our special targets.

We were, in truth, greatly outnumbered, and

potentially disastrously outgunned. Given time, good officers, and the chance to retrieve some of their specialized military equipment, these Human troops, groundhoppers or not, would be able to re-group, re-organize, and overrun us. Though I thought the Vuorrans better soldiers, if only due to their incredible reflexes, yet the Terrans could destroy us if they lost ten to our one. We could not afford a battle of attrition.

I had ordered the men to use their anti-personnel rifles (APR's) first. The troopers aimed with their laser scopes, and then squeezed the relays on the weapons. Small anti-personnel rockets leapt in pursuit of the marked targets. Once the little rockets were locked onto target, the laser guide-sights could be aimed at another enemy. The rockets would fly unerringly, and independently, to their target.

Without hesitating further, I spoke into my comm. "Comm to Cattrina. Go for it, kid! See what you can handle!

Comm to squad five. Fire at will!"

Squad five had been equipped with the heavy stuff, and vicious rockets armed with a mote of anti-matter were soon streaking towards their targets from the squad's vantage point outside of the enemy perimeter and to the right of my position. The barracks had been one of their major targets, and it exploded in sections as three separate heavy anti-matter rockets impacted.

Sentries fell from emplacements like heavy raindrops. In a moment, all officers outside or visible through windows, had fallen. Klaxon alarms started to hoot a warning, and the doors of the buildings not already destroyed were flung open by running Terran military personnel.

Many of the surviving troopers were thus outside in the open, looking for the source of the attack. They couldn't see the Vuorran troopers who lay prone under their masking cloaks, but my men and I could see the Terrans plainly. Given time, the Terrans would have probably been smart enough to get and use any vision equipment we hadn't managed to blow up.

With the right equipment in enemy hands we would be very vulnerable! Time was a luxury, however, that I didn't intend to give them. The laser fire continued, burning many Dominion troopers down as they vainly sought our locations.

As the groundhoppers dove to find shelter from my mens' withering fire of personnel rockets and laser beams, the flock of vengeful Sky Hunters soared overhead. Finding warm targets below with incorrectly identifying code signals, they dropped towards the hapless Terran soldiers. Hundreds more Dominion troops died within seconds.

I briefly thought back to when my squad was overrun by the giant TRILL, and we had called the Sky Hunters in on top of ourselves. It had saved the day, but it sure had been unnerving to have the damn things overhead trying to home in on us!

Still invisible to the panicked Terran defenders, my Vuorran troopers started to crawl forward, emptying their weapons at the soldiers and fleeing civilians alike. They relentlessly advanced. Several ran out of power for their rifles. They reached down to pick up abandoned Terran ones.

I felt somehow caught in a strange twist of time where my mind was working at an accelerated rate. The life and death struggle before me was surreal; in slow-motion. Fingers squeezed the electronic relays . . . Bodies fell to the ground . . . The savage red beams leapt instantaneously across the finite distances, defying gravity until they struck flesh . . . Screams filled the air . . . The thunderous booms of the fifth squad's exploding anti-matter rockets drowned out the frail sound of

Humans dying . . . The Vuorran wave . . . ripple, really . . . crept irresistibly forward over the piled corpses of my fellow Humans.

Each rebel soldier knew his target destination. I needed to add nothing. The Vuorran troops moved and fought as if they were battle-hardened veterans. Still cloaked, they continued to slowly advance towards those primary and pre-assigned targets. The battle was a slaughter, but it had to be for us to survive the overwhelming odds.

Suddenly a loose group of six Dominion troopers burst from the Planetary Defense building; the one building that we could not afford to destroy, and our ultimate destination. The Dominion troopers were fully armored, and obviously were a contingent of someone's personal guard, for they didn't panic.

I recognized the body armor, and felt a moment of pride. These were the toughest of a tough breed of fighting men. They were Terran Space Marines! They proved their training by weaving as they burst forth. Their helmet vision-systems were obviously tuned to the masking-cloak's wavelengths, for their fire was frugal and accurate. These were no amateur soldiers. They compared to the best I had ever seen.

"Comm to all squads! Drop to the ground! Concentrate fire on the group that just burst from Destination Alpha! . . . Now!"

Our lasers danced patterns across the ceramic armor, and sought chinks in the armor. But the targets knew enough to never stop moving, and they fired back with disconcerting accuracy. The Vuorran troopers, in their excitement, were forgetting their training. Or, perhaps, I thought, their commander should get off his ass and tell them what to do! My guys had proved themselves to be very good, but they were still green.

"Comm to all. All odd-numbered men! Revert to

your APR's. All even-numbers are to hold laser fire or only fire at helmet vision systems until there is a possible target! Commence now!"

The fire of perhaps nineteen rippling shapes paused, and then began again, re-organized. 'Damn!' I thought. The reflexes of these Vuorrans were quick! It was a good thing, for the Terran marines were also working in pairs, and they were starting to seriously cut my guys up!

The few remaining Sky Hunters hovered and paused uncertainly overhead. The multiple scramblers and screechers used by these troopers were confusing the simple brains of the little anti-personnel devices. The anti-personnel rockets fired by my men streaked in ragged volleys at the twisting and dodging group, but these guys used every trick in the book to avoid them. They were surrounded by clouds of chaff and smoke, and their suits scattered white-hot flares in all directions even as they headed right at my men.

Our only hope for a knock-out punch was to burst the ceramic armor with an explosive rocket, and then let the lasers get to work on the metal choblom armor beneath. If my troops didn't get past these guys soon, our element of surprise would be lost. Even now, a large fleet of Vuorran 'pirate' vessels, in reality mainly stolen Dominion freighters girded with a modicum of armor plating and jury-rigged missile systems, would be breaking out of hyperspace only a few light-seconds away.

If the Vuorran fleet had only to face the small naval contingent in orbit above, the Vuorran High Command had calculated that we had a fighting chance for success. Against the combined battle systems of the Dominion naval vessels and the planet's Ground Defense . . . well, the 'puter projections weren't good.

My 'puter informed me that there were now seventeen Vuorran troopers alive and functioning, including me. We were wearing down the cluster of

Dominion marines, but it might cost us a few more men.

"Comm to all. When you can, turn cloaking devices off. Use flares and chaff. Now! Close for hand combat!"

I really didn't know what else to do. We were losing two Vuorrans for every Dominion marine that fell. Our reliance on the cloaking system had suddenly become a liability. The Terran marines were cutting us up from behind the screen of chaff, smoke and flares. Long delay was, for us, certain defeat. We had to get in to that building, and get in it now! There were many more troops somewhere on this planet, and if they arrived, we were dead!

The Vuorran troopers, the cloaking devices off but the smoke and chaff making them hard to clearly see, rolled forward in a tiny tidal wave. Cattrina, her two guards, and I all joined them in a second little wave. Either we got in now, or we died!

The first wave of bodies hit the Dominion marines like an avalanche. The Terran troops were larger and stockier, but I knew from experience that the 'puny' Vuorrans had incredible speed and tremendous strength. We were well matched. Both groups continued firing until we could touch each other, and then we grabbed and kicked.

"Comm to Cattrina! Cattrina! Can you do anything to stop the slaughter? Can you adjust their minds?"

"No, Timm! Later, yes . . . but not now! They are battle crazed. I can do nothing."

Damn! I had hoped that we could spare them. We could use such good men on our side. We had no time to play games now, however. Too much was riding on this attack!

"Comm to all. Take 'em down! Kill 'em!"

The Terrans stood for a few seconds more, surrounded by a swirl of smaller but similarly armored Vuorrans, but they were eventually overwhelmed, and they went down under the sheer weight of numbers. Hands twisted the system controls and pulled at the armor, and the men were suddenly helpless.

True to their conditioning, however, the Terran marines did not cease struggling for one second. The Vuorran troopers peeled back part of the armor and finished the marines one by one with their dirks.

It was time to move. Now a total of seventeen, including me and Cattrina, we charged the main building. There was no more serious resistance. The few civilians we encountered fled at our approach.

We entered the nerve center for Planetary Defense to find only a few technicians. Several seemed to have been received the 'Emperor's Kiss', for while they seemed to want to run, they were unable. I well knew how they felt, having been brainwashed myself. I knew the pain had been excruciating when I tried to follow my common sense. A Vourran psychologist had once explained it to me. He said that the Dominion brain-twisters had replaced the parental voices that constituted my Freudian superego with much sharper ones that told me that duty to the Emperor came before all personal feelings. Death became preferable to disobedience.

The volatile mixture of common sense coming into conflict with a stated order had been pain . . . intense and crippling. Only when I followed the 'Emperor's voice' did the pain diminish. Well did I know it. Cattrina had saved me from the agony of such a conflict when I first caught up with her on Croton III.

I spoke into my helmet mike. "Comm to all. Hold the technicians. Only kill if necessary! Cattrina, we may need them! Can you see what you can do with them?"

My faithful troopers sprang forward to knock the technicians to the ground. Once they were securely pinned, Cattrina moved forward and placed her hands on their brows. I could see the pain on her face as she read their auras, and then attempted to 'smooth' the 'knots'.

Several of the technicians relaxed under her ministrations, and the men let them go. Three others would not, or could not, and after Cattrina nodded a negative, the troopers injected heavy doses of tranquillizers to incapacitate them.

Although the entire attack so far had taken perhaps three minutes or less, it seemed to me like hours had passed. I knew that this was due to my heightened senses. Within moments the resistance in the center had ceased.

Cattrina straightened up from her task with the captives, and headed for the main 'puter banks. I could see the terrible pain mirrored in her eyes, but I could do nothing to help her. I knew that she felt the pain of each person in her vicinity, and lived it with them. She intensely felt each death. I had wanted to give her some endorphins, but she had told me that anything that blocked the mental pain also blocked her sensing ability.

Already psychically exhausted, she staggered to the main command terminals and placed her hands on the controls. I knew that the gesture was unnecessary. She had shown an ability to control computers as long as she was in the area of their electro-magnetic field. Still, the physical contact was symbolic, and seemed to allow her to better focus her own mental energy. Although I could see nothing, I knew that her electro-magnetic field, her 'aura', flared and merged with the computer. Where there were conflicts, she smoothed them, until her aura and the 'puter's began to match. Once they were in accord, the 'puter was ours! That was what we had to do this day; or die. The fate of our own battle fleet, as well as the tens of thousands of Vuorran captives on the planet, depended on it!

The struggle was much briefer than when she had helped me seize control of our purloined navy vessel, but I could see that the effort was immense. Fifteen troopers and her lover stood waiting. Our battle was done for the moment. Cattrina struggled alone.

Suddenly I realized that there was no one on watch. The troopers might be finished for now, but the battle was not yet done. I assumed my mantle as commander.

"All right you lazy slugs! Party time is over! Squad leader! I want defensive positions set up in the outside hall and at the windows. You guys hit the Terrans hard, but they got a lot more troops than we do, and they're going to arrive here at any time. Move it!"

We had attained our first objective, but I was worried. If our ships did not destroy the Dominion fleet overhead, we would very soon be fighting a lop-sided battle that only had one possible ending.

After making a quick circuit of our little perimeter, I returned to the side of my Princess. She sat on the floor, her back propped against a table leg, but she smiled at me.

"We have won a great victory today, my Major! The planetary defenses are 'down'! The 'puters will not attack the Terran Space Fleet, but neither will they order an attack against our fleet. It is the best that I can do."

What she said was great news! Hundreds of missiles were poised on the ground against any kind of planetary attack. Many more were probably hidden on asteroids and moons of the planetary system, as well as any energy weapons the Dominion High Command had chosen to put into space or on the land in case of just such an attack as ours. All would be interconnected to this very nerve center. That is why the Vurroan High Command had risked the very valuable princess's hide.

Cattrina's news meant that the entire defensive system was now inoperative. I knew with a grim certainty that the rebel fleet, relatively unarmored as it was, could never have prevailed against such planetary defenses. With the planetary defenses down, the Vuorran fleet only had to face the small naval contingent in orbit.

"Conder! Caseter! Condylan! Get over to the 'puter controls! See if you can get us a hologram of the planetary system. Let's see how our fleet is doing!"

Only Caseter and Condylan stepped forward. I hadn't realized it, but Conder hadn't made to it the command room. I realized he must have gone down in the fierce firefight with the Marines. He had been the best of the 'puter experts, but he was also obviously dead or missing.

I didn't have time to mourn his absence. The 'puter expert had been a friend, and I would miss him, but now was not the time to think about his death! There would be time enough if we survived the day.

Cattrina's voice was weak, but she was still alert. "Timm, the 'puter will now accept your voice commands."

I tried her suggestion. "Battle computer! Do you hear me?"

"I hear you, Centurion. What are your wishes?"

Even here, tens of light-years from my home sector, the 'puter banks had my personal ID and personnel data. Incredible!

"Please project the near-space area on your holographic box. Use parameters that allow me to see both space fleets simultaneously."

"As you wish, Centurion."

Almost instantly the projection box lit up. I could see a slice of the planet we sat on, and several red lights indicated the relative position of the Dominion naval contingent. Several planetary diameters out, a green series of dots had coalesced. The Vuorran battle fleet was here!

I ordered each squad to split. Half were to hold their posts in anticipation of a renewal of hostilities. The rest stood riveted in front of the projection box.

We were watching history in the making. The first Vuorran-Dominion space battle in history was unfolding before us. All our lives depended on the outcome.

The projection was on much too large a scale for me to see clearly what was happening, but I knew the Vuorran battle plan, and I watched it unfolding. Over thirty ships formed up in a thin cylindrical formation. I knew that in the midst of that cylinder was one of our kilometer-long particle-beam projectors. Thirty ships in harness! The flow of electrons from thirty fusion systems could project an incredible beam; hopefully greater than anything anyone in the Dominion had ever seen.

A second and broader cylinder of ships formed around the first. These were the armored freighters, each loaded with large numbers of missiles. The Vuorran fleet was unable to go head to head with Dominion battle-wagons, since we did not have the energy shielding, the massive armor, and the many varied beam weapons.

We COULD, however, put our automated factories to work, and we had. The fleet carried thousands of atomic and anti-matter warheads. Most would not penetrate the battleships' armor, but there were so many that some would. It only took one to destroy even a Dominion dreadnought, and that was not what the rebel fleet was facing here.

The great beam lanced out at the Terran fleet. The Dominion ships were warships, and as such, capable of projecting strong energy shields. No shield, however, could long hold against the concentrated hell of electrons that flowed from the giant Vuorran weapon. One Dominion ship, and then another was struck by the intense beam. The energy shields held for milli-seconds, and then suddenly flared. Moments later the target ship simply disappeared.

Myriad tiny green dots moved outwards from our Vuorran fleet. I knew that the dots heralded the launching of the vast array of atomic and anti-matter rockets. I had stolen the idea from the TRILL, except that they had used manned vessels. In spite of the vast superiority of the

Dominion fleet at the First Space Battle against the TRILL, the many kamikaze TRILL scout ships had almost cost the Terrans the battle.

The tiny robotic brains of the Vuorran rockets were cheap and disposable. The Vuorran High Command prayed that our massive launchings would overwhelm the Terran ship defenses. If nothing else, it took attention away from the great particle beam projector. That was, after all, highly vulnerable.

The massive Vuorran attack was utterly unexpected, and devastatingly effective. One after the other, the lights that represented the Dominion naval ships winked out in the Holographic box. Within minutes, a dozen ships and thousands of men had their molecules and very atoms scattered into the void of space.

I felt sick at the death, but I knew that there had been no chance of surrender. The 'Emperor's Kiss' ensured that the Humans would fight to the last. Surrender was not an option after the brain-twisters were through with you.

The holographic box indicated that the victorious Vuorran vessels were entering the planet's atmosphere. I, Cattrina, and our stalwart Vuorran soldiers were continuing to hold the master defense 'puter center that we had so bloodily seized.

There was sporadic weapons fire from the remaining Dominion groundhoppers who had survived our original savage onslaught, but no serious threats had showed up as yet. I well knew that the majority of the Vuorran vessels were headed directly for the slave camps on the other continent.

There was no telling what the Dominion conditioning would force the Terrans to do when they realized that they had lost the planet. Thus, the first priority had been to get in as fast as possible and rescue as many Vuorrans as possible.

I had agreed that there should only be a small task

force sent to rescue us. If a large Terran ground force arrived at the 'puter Center before the rescuers arrived, well, that had been the risk of the operation. I would only regret the death of my beautiful princess Cattrina. The last adult member of the Vuorran royal family known to be alive and free, she was a powerful symbol for the Vuorran people. Even more important, she possessed some special skills in telepathy that made her absolutely unique, and needed on this forsaken planet. Only she had been capable of shutting down the Dominion ground defenses.

I well knew that if we had been unable to shut the master battle computer down, the Vuorran fleet would have stood no chance at all. As it was, an overconfident Dominion naval contingent had presumably been relying on the powerful planetary defenses, and our little Vuorran expedition had wrought a miracle. Now all we had to do was to live to enjoy it!

The Center was coming under more and more fire from the groundhoppers who had dug in, in the very positions that my troopers had so recently occupied.

I was contemplating ordering an evacuation in spite of the dangers. The anti-matter charges were in place. The life span of the building and its 'puters could be measured in minutes, when I heard the roar of a bulbous vessel displacing air at a great speed. I spoke to my comm. I dared not look out of the window.

"Comm to Vuorran ship channel! Come in ship! I repeat, come in! Identify yourself."

"Good morning, Major! I understand that you would like a lift today. Is now satisfactory, or would you like me to come back later?"

I would have known that conceited voice anywhere! It could only belong to my purloined naval vessel computer.

"It's about time that you showed up, Tinhead! Use your heavy weapons and clear the perimeter! We are under heavy fire here! Do you think that you can handle that?"

"Major, don't I always come through for you? Your wish is my command!"

Whatever my annoyance at the flippancy Tinhead was exhibiting, I knew that it had been specifically designed for just such operations. Though Cattrina and I had flown it half-way across the galaxy, and it had proved to be a capable craft, yet it was really a ground-support vessel. As such it excelled. We could suddenly hear heavy weapons fire, and the room lit up, though it was daylight outside; with the long bursts of intense energy released by the ship.

Suddenly our little force was no longer besieged. All weapons fire ceased, and the globular vessel settled gently to the ground right by the main door of the building.

"Comm to all! Okay ladies! Make sure that the detonators are set for two minutes max in case we can't trigger them by remote! Run for the ship one at a time! O.K. Tinhead, I know you're listening. Open the door now! . . . Squad One to four! Move it! . . . Squad five, Screen the Princess! . . . Go now! O.K. Tinhead, I'm last. When I'm aboard, button up, and lift. I think we're going to get a lot more company here."

I made my break for the open and inviting ship transport portal. There was no firing as I crossed the short distance. The ship's suppressive fire had seriously dented any organized resistance. Still, I knew that at any time someone might dig up a weapon that could destroy the entire ship. It was time to get the hell out of there!

"Tinhead, lift to a thousand meters, then blow the explosives. Do it now! After you have managed that, head for the fleet rendezvous. All shielding is to be at max just as soon as the building blows. Understood?"

"Of course, Major! Done even as you speak. The explosives have blown, and my sensors indicate that parts of the building are rapidly catching up to us. May I express my deep sorrow for the loss of such a powerful computer. It is truly sad to see . . ."

"Tinhead! Are all shields up? Are we on the way to rendezvous with the transport fleet?"

"Of course, Major! I just wanted to take this opportunity to point out . . ."

"Tinhead, silence is golden. Please pretend you are worth something!"

"Well, I never!"

I looked out of the nearest port and realized that the ship was indeed on its way somewhere, and quickly. I knew that the ship was capable of endless multi-tasking, but it still scared me to have it chatting when I thought it should be concentrating on more important things. I wondered if Tinhead was getting senile from an excess of time and radiation, but I hesitated to have it replaced or re-programmed. The obnoxious thing actually did seem to like me.

Much writing starts as a challenge. I set myself a difficult goal, and then find a way for my hero to achieve it. How can a small band of alien rebels take on the galaxy's greatest military power and win? That was this story's challenge.

This story tells the adventures of a human military officer who finds love and a new destiny with an alien princess. Freed of his military brainwashing, he joins the Vuorrans, an alien race targeted for annihilation by an evil Terran emperor. He soon finds himself commander of a rag-tag force of alien civilians, fighting the greatest empire in the galaxy.

Eventually, this and other short stories became chapters, and the whole eventually transmogrified into a Science Fiction novel, The Vuorran Pogrom.

12. "STICKS AND STONES"

The Emperor's Chief Advisor bowed gracefully the requisite three times, prostrated himself before the master of the entire known universe, and waited for permission to move. The silver-haired man, leaning back on his ornate throne, nodded politely and spoke with his melodious voice.

"Rise, Sir Reginald, and tell me what is on your mind

today."

"Thank you, Majesty. There is one item that caught my attention this morning."

"Then speak up, Advisor."

"Sire, it has come to my attention that the Arizians have placed an order for one thousand Evan's hyper-drive warp generators."

The Arizians . . . hmm . . . There is no way those second class inhabitants of a third class star system could use an extra hundred warp generators, let alone a thousand."

"Exactly, Your Majesty! They are clearly fronting for the Vuorran rebels. We must move fast and punish the bastards!"

The Emperor smiled. "Whoa, Sir Reginald. Let us think this through a little more carefully."

The advisor looked puzzled, but he merely nodded. "As you command, Majesty."

"I applaud your eagerness, Sir Reginald, but just what exactly would the Vuorrans do with a thousand warp generators?"

"A thousand Vuorran warships could probably bring commerce throughout the Dominion to a complete halt, Majesty. They have done pretty damn well with the few dozen ships they have managed to hijack so far."

"No doubt true, Sir Reginald, but what is the cost of constructing a single trader?"

"Close to a million universal credits, Sire."

"And a small battle-cruiser?"

"Closer to three."

"So if we let the Vuorrans purchase the Evan's hyper-drive warp generators, then they would have to spend a minimum of a billion, and perhaps as much as three billion credits, before they would actually have a functional fleet."

"They might choose to not build a thousand,

Majesty."

"Then why buy a thousand warp generators?"

"Perhaps stockpiling for future use, Sire?"

"Sir Reginald, the last surviving Vuorrans in all the universe are hiding on some dirtball somewhere out on the Rim. Their very survival depends on them successfully hiding from our navy scouts. They have no economy, nor an industrial capacity worthy of the name. They do not have a billion credits, and no one in their right mind would loan them that sum."

Sir Reginald sighed. "They have stolen a great deal of money on their pirate raids, Majesty."

The Emperor laughed out loud. "So they will pay us for the warp generators with our own money."

"Sire, with all due respect, I fail to find the humor in that."

"Relax, Sir Reginald, and let us think this through a little further.

First, we give the Vuorrans the warp generators they covet. Cite national emergency and charge the Arizians double. We have a monopoly, so they will hardly be in a position to argue. How is the economy doing on Albacrom II?"

"Disastrously, Majesty. There are few orders for new space ships when the Vuorrans are pillaging and looting the space lanes."

"So if we let the sale go through, we provide several man-centuries of labor for a planet that is suffering massive unemployment due to the rebellion. The Vuorrans are forced to go on to a massive industrialization drive to build the ships. All their money and effort will have to go towards that single goal. And don't forget; each time they build a factory or are forced to purchase a ship part from us, they leave a potential trail. Even if we don't find them, we bankrupt them."

"I understand, your Majesty, but we also loose a

pirate fleet a dozen times larger than what is plaguing us now."

The Emperor grinned. "Of course. And then the colonial planets that were growing restless under our paternal hand are reminded of the value of the Dominion fleet. And if the furry little bastards leave as much as one single clue for us, then the Vuorrans are finished!"

"I hear and obey, Majesty."

The emperor smiled. "But you do not agree."

"I accept your logic, Majesty, but I would be less-than-honest if I did not tell you that I think the risk is too great."

"That is why you are my chief advisor, Sir Reginald. I am surrounded by sycophants. I need an honest man to guide me. Oh, Sir Reginald, before you go, I have a last question. Are the warp generators permanently sealed?"

"Yes, Majesty. They have been carefully designed. To open them is to destroy them."

"Excellent. Then tell the design engineers that I want flawed generators produced."

"Flawed, Sire? How exactly?"

"I want the generators to have a life expectancy of no more than a hundred jumps."

"Majesty, they generally have a life expectancy of over a billion jumps."

The Emperor grinned. "I know. In a couple of months from now, I want a lot of Vuorrans to make a jump somewhere, and then discover the design flaw first hand."

Sir Reginald grinned in return." It will be my pleasure, Sire! I will see to it personally."

Admiral-of-the-Fleet Bennington stood on the bridge of the Planet-Crusher H.R.M. Hermes. At his side stood the young nephew of the Emperor himself, and through the view ports the planet Nirvana, known throughout the universe as the Emperor's private residence, turned serenely.

The young boy's voice piped irritatingly through the bridge. "Admiral, what is such a great emergency that you have brought fully half of the fleet's Planet-Crushers into this space sector?"

"The dastardly Vuorrans have threatened Nirvana, your Highness."

"Nirvana is known throughout the universe as the emperor's personal residence, Admiral! What foul creatures dare to threaten the emperor's personal domain?"

"The Vuorrans are a cowardly feline race, Highness."

"Are they mad at my uncle?"

"Some months ago your revered uncle, long may he reign in peace, ordered the interdiction of the Vuorran home world, and the arrest and extermination of any Vuorrans found in the Terran Dominion."

"Were the Vuorrans bad people?"

"It is not mine to question, Highness. That your uncle ordered it is enough for me."

The thin face stared haughtily at the admiral. "But why?"

"Highness, your uncle said that the Vuorrans had become a source of serious danger to the Terran Dominion."

"Then why were they not crushed like my uncle ordered?"

"They were, Highness. Many were killed. Millions more were arrested and are being held both in concentration camps and on their home planet."

The young prince's voice became suddenly shriller. "Then why, Admiral, are we standing here fearing for the safety of the emperor's residential planet? And just how did the Vuorrans manage to threaten a planet which has half of the universe's Planet-Busters circling it?"

"It appears to have been surprisingly easy, Highness. The idea is no doubt another cute trick from that renegade

Centurion known as Timm Bruce. The Vuorrans snuck into the asteroid belt and surreptitiously mounted rocket engines on thousands of rocks of varying sizes."

"And just why would that endanger Nirvana, Admiral?"

"By various slow burns, the asteroids were all re-directed at the planet, Highness."

"Will the asteroids collide with Nirvana, Admiral?"

"They would have, Highness, except that the burns were detected in time for us to assemble the fleet."

"But if you know they are coming, and you have enough sheer firepower to destroy a sun, just what is the problem, Admiral?"

The Admiral sighed. The first asteroids were coming into range very shortly, and he would have dearly liked to focus on the last minute details. It was not expedient to ignore the emperor's nephew, however.

"We know how many approach, and their trajectory, Highness, but we must make sure that no large asteroids enter the planet's atmosphere.

"What danger are these few rocks to the planet, Admiral?"

"Highness, there are several hundred of them, and most of the asteroids are over two-hundred meters in diameter."

"Won't the asteroids just burn up in the atmosphere?"

"You are right, Highness, to a point."

The boy showed a flash of his famous family temper. "I am either right or wrong, Admiral. Which is it?"

"Past a certain size, an asteroid will not burn up in the upper atmosphere of the planet, but will hit the ground, or, equally disastrous, explode near the planet's surface. The resulting burst of energy is equivalent of hundreds of fusion bombs. If such a thing happened, there is even a chance that the lives of the members of the royal court could be at risk."

"You said that the Vuorrans were interned. Just who dares do such a thing?"

"Highness, it is unfortunately true that some ragged remains of the race escaped the galaxy-wide sweep and found a hidden sanctuary. Allied with some enemies of the Dominion, they have gradually begun to strike back."

"How can a few thousand, or even a few million, aliens hurt my uncle's Dominion? Didn't you say they were just some kind of giant cats?"

"They are an ancient race evolved from felines, Highness. The Vuorran fugitives have stolen merchant vessels, and thus have gradually built up a fleet. This pirate fleet now attacks the length and breadth of the Dominion's star lanes."

"Admiral, you have half of the universe's Planet-Crushers floating out here in space. Surely just a few of these flying moons could take care of a few rocks?"

"Highness, the beams from a Planet-Crusher battlewagon can overload the strongest force fields in seconds, and then slice an enemy vessel into pieces. Once an enemy hull is breached, the ship is generally finished as a fighting vessel."

"Admiral, I am aware of this. What has this to do with a few asteroids?"

"If your Highness would be patient, I would be pleased to explain it to you. What happens when we carve deep into a hurtling rock?"

"I don't know. I suppose it melts."

"If you are lucky, you might split it. Now you have two enormous rocks hurtling towards Nirvana."

"I think, Admiral, that you are trying to tell me that an asteroid is harder to destroy than a ship."

"Exactly, your Highness. That is why there will be several levels to our defense. Any asteroids that make it past the Planet-Crushers will be vaporized or broken up by either Ground Defense or the rest of the fleet."

The royal nephew started to look alarmed. "Is it really possible that any asteroids will make it to the surface, Admiral?"

"Highness, this fleet is probably the most powerful in all the universe, and I have reinforced it with the full weight of the Planetary Defense System. And just to be sure, I have called in contingents of several other sector fleets. I want to be absolutely sure that there is no chance of any large asteroids entering the planet's atmosphere."

"It is as well that you did, Admiral. My mother says that Uncle will order executions if so much as a single rock hits the ground."

The admiral sighed. "Your Highness looks tired. Perhaps now you would like a nap?"

"Don't be annoying, Admiral. I intend to stay on the bridge and watch how you handle the asteroids. My uncle tells me that one day I will be a great military commander."

"I have no doubt, your Highness."

The Admiral-of-the-Fleet watched the tiny lights of his holographic projection-tank slowly coalesce into his master battle-plan. He felt a trifle nervous, knowing that the Emperor himself would be scanning the skies; watching his fleet at work.

The Admiral knew that the boy's mother was not fooling. The tiniest error on his part could cost him his head. The Emperor was not known as a forgiving man. Yet the old warrior had done all that could be done. He had even reinforced the fleet far past what the 'puters had said were necessary to deal effectively with the approaching danger.

The boy had a puzzled expression on his face. He interrupted the admiral again. "Admiral, is it likely that your fleet would have picked up the telltale signs of reaction-drive emissions?"

"The engines were programmed to burn slow and

pretty far out, but yes, I would have to say that it is likely that the emissions would eventually be spotted."

"If the Vuorrans know you have a strong fleet in orbit, and expect you to spot the engine emissions in lots of time to prepare, why did they bother to go to all this trouble?"

The admiral looked at the youngster with a new respect. It was a valid question, and one he had asked himself many times. The Vuorrans were few, and savagely hunted. Vast armadas of navy vessels were scouring distant star systems; ferreting out the last Vuorran outpost. The final destruction of the Vuorran race was imminent. Why go to all this trouble when the result of the attack was a foregone conclusion?

"You are very astute, Highness. Something about this whole action continues to bother me, too. But it makes little difference now. We are committed.

Please come and watch the action, Highness. The asteroids approach the 'kill zone', and my crewmen eagerly await the opportunity to show you and your uncle what they can do."

The first battlewagon opened fire when the command ship's 'puter determined that the optimal moment had arrived. Electrical systems large enough to power entire moons crackled, and hellish bursts of energy leapt across the void. The giant rocks in their path exploded or flowed liquid.

The terrible beams were followed by thousands of anti-matter mines that were themselves capable of considerable destruction. The Emperor and his royal court watched the celestial fireworks from their vantage point on the surface thousands of kilometers below.

The Admiral did not notice, but some of the rocks burst apart before any missile struck or energy beam carved into them. The automated 'puter-controlled defenses ignored these smaller pieces, as they were well below the threshold size of danger.

The Dominion Naval Command knew that they could not literally destroy all of the hurtling rock mass. There were cubic kilometers of it; all targeted at the planet spinning majestically below.

The Admiral's instructions were to ensure that no piece large enough to be dangerous made it past the wall of ships. The atmosphere itself was capable of handling pieces up to twenty meters in diameter.

While the Admiral worried about his ships, yet he knew that their shields could handle small debris and even middle-sized rocks. The ring of giant Planet-Crushers were systematically carving up the larger pieces, and the waiting smaller vessels were capable of taking care of anything that made it past the Planet-Crushers.

The carefully constructed pieces of 'debris' hurtled onwards towards the battle fleet, each piece now small enough to be ignored by the ship 'puters. The anti-matter bombs they carried, however, were programmed to explode if they hit an energy shield of any kind.

Many of the chunks of rock were sliced again by lasers, or hit the wall of space mines, but some managed to hit ship energy deflectors. The bombs exploded in awesome silence, hurling intense bursts of light and energy against the shields.

The Planet-Crushers had massive enough power generators and capacitors that they were capable of absorbing the hellish energy released, but the smaller vessels could not, and their shields went down. A ship without shields lasted only seconds in the avalanche of rocks and bombs raining down on them. Even the larger vessels were hard-pressed to handle multiple bursts.

The Admiral was in shock to see several vessels of his fleet suddenly explode. He did not, however, hesitate for a moment.

"Commodore. Relay these commands to all ships.

First command. Captains are to hold their position at all costs!

Second command. Each vessel is instructed to beam any rocks that might come into contact with their energy shields. Our furry little friends seem to have put their own anti-matter mines on some of the smaller rocks! It is vital that the anti-matter mines are triggered before they hit the ship shields.

Third command. Launch all marines forthwith."

The thin little face swiveled to focus on the admiral again. "Admiral, why are you launching your soldiers into space?"

The admiral sighed. "Highness, the Dominion marines, mounted on their scooters and armed with their own anti-matter missiles, will be able to multiply my effective force several-fold."

"Admiral, they don't have energy shields and there is terrible radiation out there. How will they survive?"

The admiral's face was sweaty, in spite of the air conditioning on the bridge. "Highness, they wear radiation suits. For some, the radiation and rocks may possibly be lethal, but we will pick up the survivors later and treat them. They are soldiers. It is their job to die, if necessary, in defense of their Emperor. Unfortunately, it appears that this is exactly what some of them must do today."

The emperor's nephew called again in a nasal tone. "Admiral, what are these new red dots in the holographic tank?"

The admiral sighed. "Highness, you heard me tell the marines to launch. They should be visible about now."

"Admiral, I am not stupid! The marines show in blue. These are something else!"

Counting slowly to control his anger, the admiral walked over to the holo-tank and stared into it. Even as he watched, more and more strange vessels burst out of hyper-space not far from where the Dominion battle fleet floated in formation.

"Holy shit! Commodore, what the hell are these red dots?"

"Unknown, sir! Sensors indicate no life-forms and the readings make no sense. They are NOT vessels, whatever else they are."

"They are dropping out of hyper-space, Commodore. That would make them ships to me!"

"Admiral, nobody in their right mind drops out of hyper-space this close to a planet! It's suicidal! Besides, the readings are like nothing I have ever seen before!"

"What are you talking about?"

"Sensors indicate that the objects are solid. Whatever they are, though, they are none-the-less dangerous, sir! Their mass and speed is enormous, and it is taking a whole lot of energy to damage them! It's like they're rocks flying through hyper-space!"

The admiral screamed to his commanders. "Order the puters to recalculate the firing pattern! I want those new objects, whatever the hell they are, carved up and destroyed before they're on top of us! No doubt the little furry bastards have also covered them with anti-matter mines!"

The commodore stood at attention. "Admiral, recalculating. It will take a few minutes to destroy them all!"

"That's not good enough! You have the most powerful fleet in the universe. What is the problem!?"

"Admiral, we are hitting them, but more just keep coming!"

"Whatever the hell they are, they are a danger to Nirvana and to our Emperor! They must be stopped at all costs!"

The Commodore tried again. "Admiral, if we focus just on them, some of the bigger asteroids will make it past us!"

The Admiral glared at his subordinate. "The decision has been made. Just do it, Commodore."

With despair in his heart, the Admiral ordered the 'puter to activate his personal direct-link to the Emperor. "Your Majesty, we are facing an unprecedented attack here. It is my duty to ask you to evacuate the royal court as quickly as possible . . . yes, Majesty, you can try me for anything you want, after the battle."

The admiral blanched. A terrifying thought had just entered his head.

"Commodore, why are we forbidden to drop out of hyper-space within 40,000 kilometers of a planet?"

"It is suicidal, sir. I can only think of one time when it has been done. We overrode our own 'puters and did it once against the Khazers."

"And the result?"

"We beat the crap out of them, but we lost almost half of our ships to collisions."

"So the risk to the ships and crew is too great? Sweet merciful God!"

Both the royal nephew and the commodore stared at the admiral. At last the commodore spoke. "Admiral, what is it?!"

"If you were shooting big rocks through hyper-space instead of twenty million credit battleships, and you didn't care how many you lost, you could drop them right on top of a fleet."

"Admiral, two solid objects cannot be in the same place at the same time. It is an irrefutable law of nature!"

The royal nephew had watched the interplay of emotions flit across the two men's faces. At last he could stand it no longer.

"Admiral, I command you to tell me what you are talking about!"

"It is simple, Highness. You may be about to witness

the destruction of a good part of the greatest fleet in the universe."

The nephew was now thoroughly frightened. "What is going to happen?"

"It is just possible that the Vuorrans have stripped some of their surplus ships of their Evan's generators and used them to throw some big rocks right on top of us."

The Commodore looked grim. "Admiral, they may hurt us a little, but they only have a couple of dozen ships in total and there is no way in hell they could produce their own generators. How many ships can they afford to lose . . . oh shit!"

The admiral's voice thundered. "What is it, Commodore? Speak up, man!"

The Commodore spoke in a wooden voice. "There was a report, sir, of a thousand Evan's hyper-drive warp generators being seized by Vuorran raiders in a daring raid on an Arizian convoy less than a month ago."

"And what would you do with a thousand Evan's warp generators?"

"If I was the enemy, and I had more Evan's warp generators then I know what to do with, I just might use them to throw rocks right on top of the fleet. The fleet would have no time to react. Even a small rock inside of our ship's energy screens has the potential to destroy the entire ship."

"And if it materialized right in the ship?"

The Commodore spoke in awe. "God help us! But first I would ensure that the fleet is immobilized."

"Like we would be if we were concentrating on a hail of giant asteroids."

"If we stay we die, and if we move, the emperor's personal planet is severely damaged."

The royal nephew stared accusingly at the admiral. "How would these Vuorrans know where you would place your fleet, Admiral? Has my uncle been betrayed?"

The admiral sighed. "That would not have been necessary, Highness. It is all a simple mathematical exercise. If you know the trajectories of the asteroids, and you know the basic makeup of the fleet, you just put your 'puter to work, and it comes up with an optimal plan."

Even as the admiral spoke, the holo-tank suddenly filled with hundreds more colored lights. Some hurtling rocks dropped out of hyper-space directly in front of the ships, while others appeared right within the fleet formation. Alarms signaled that a few giant rocks appeared right at the periphery of the planet's atmosphere, well past the last circle of naval vessels.

The admiral watched the holographic tank for a few moments, and then let out his anger in one burst. "Shit!"

He took several long breaths, and then turned again to the Commodore. "Casualties?"

"Several Planet-Crushers have already been damaged by a combination of rocks and anti-matter mines. Others have simply ceased to exist. It is presumed that rocks materialized right within the ships."

"And?"

"Two solid objects cannot coexist in the same place at the same time, Admiral."

The admiral smiled at the royal nephew, and then reactivated his link with the Emperor. "Majesty, you have only minutes before first impact. Evacuate now!"

Without even bothering to hear the response, he flicked his personal comm to all-call. "Rear-Admiral, Smits, Planetary Defense is now responsible for any asteroids that make to the planet's atmosphere. Good shooting and good luck! As for my fleet captains, your instructions have not changed. You are to stand and fight!"

The nephew tugged on the admiral's sleeve. The old man looked down at the frightened face.

"Admiral, I want to go back to my uncle. What is

going on out there?"

"It's quite simple, Your Highness. You will have to stay with us for just a little bit longer. The Commodore just said it. The most powerful fleet in the universe is being pasted by a bunch of rocks!"

"Are we all going to die?"

"Highness, we are going to lose a lot of ships, and some asteroids are going to make it past us. Some of the fleet will likely survive. You may be sure we will do our duty. We will hold our position at all costs."

This is another short story that escaped from my pen back when I was a university student. As a teenager, I remember lying in bed and breaking into a sweat when I heard the late night droning of jet engines. I lived in a world where hundreds of planes, both American and Soviet, flew endlessly through the dark skies with their terrible cargo of nuclear weapons. The death of civilization as I knew it often seemed very close. In retrospect, it seems amazing how stimulated my creative drive became when the alternative was to read boring text books.

13. THE ATOM

In the midst of nothingness, a space craft slid gently from n-space, and suddenly was physically there. Far below the scintillating mass of polished duraluminum, a blue and green planet hung in the void of space.

Captain Angus Hawk, tall and thin almost to emaciation, looked once more at his panel of sensory dials. He double-checked the calculations for the final descent. Although this was the thirteenth planet in just over two hundred home-planet rotations, and the descent only signaled the beginning of the real work, the crew pressed their eager faces to the view-screens like little children. Each wanted to better see this alien world that appeared so like their own. Meanwhile, unconcernedly, the green-girded planet continued its slow rotation.

As the ship approached one hundred kilometers and the Master Navigation computer beeped a gentle warning. Captain Hawk punched manual override and gently eased backward on the retrorocket control.

"Here we go, folks. Strap in and stasis shields on! We're going down on the chemicals. Just sit back and let your favorite Captain bring you down safe and sound."

Even as he engaged in his ritualistic patter, his deft fingers danced on the Master Control Board. He didn't even hear the rude sound from his Second Officer. Fiery jets of flame leapt ahead of the plunging globe.

In spite of the enormous pull of gravity on the craft, the roaring energy jets soon slowed the craft's plunge to a speed the rapidly heating metal plates could handle. His skill brought the craft to the surface as lightly as if it were a filmy bubble, and not a several thousand-ton mass of steel and aluminum, lead and plastic. The very silence of the crew served as a compliment to their commander's skills, since he well-remembered the vocal outbursts that had followed his somewhat less than perfect landing in the atmospheric maelstrom of Helicon VII.

Crewmen who had yet to tire of new landfalls broke free from their stasis shields and eagerly raced to their ground stations. Even Captain Hawk could spare only a few moments to hungrily eye the lithe figure of Chief Physician Tanya Crow as she hurried to hers. Even dressed in her loose-fitting work overalls, he found her erotic and exciting. As he watched her perch at her station and begin precise manipulations of her station controls, he thought lustful thoughts.

Damn, he thought. I sure wish she would give me the time of the day. She does stir my nesting instincts. He shook his head in a vain effort to dislodge the inappropriate thoughts that had slipped uninvited into his head and broken his concentration. He was ultimately responsible for the safety of not only the ship, but of every man and woman aboard. He couldn't afford to be distracted by any female, whatever her attractions. The sooner the crewmen ran their assigned tests, the sooner they could unbutton the ship and start the real exploration.

This planet looked like a real winner. With luck, they would not have to wear uncomfortable protective suits and breathe their stale tanked air. With a sigh, the captain forced his attention to focus again on the task at hand. He called out to the various stations.

"Electronics. What's your report?"

"I've scanned all band widths, Captain. I'm not picking up anything other than natural electrical static."

"Atmospherics?"

"I read an A2 Plus Oxygen atmosphere, sir. It looks pretty good. I am picking up a surprisingly high background radiation count, but it's not at a lethal level."

"O.K., guys. If Medical says it's a go, then you can head out at dawn."

Captain Hawk waited impatiently for the dulcet tones of Tanya's voice to respond. "A preliminary scan of the sample microorganisms I've located so far indicates that they are not inimical to our bio-systems. Give me a couple more hours to sample some macro-organisms, and I'll have enough of a DNA analysis to tell if there is likely to be any sort of a health risk for us. I should be able to have a comprehensive report completed for you by first light."

The captain looked stern. "You heard the Doctor. Nobody goes outside or so much as cracks an air seal until I have her complete report on my computer screen and she gives the word. Is that understood by all of you keeners?"

Once Tanya Crow, Chief Medical Officer aboard the

scout vessel, gave her OK, the preliminary ground-exploration crew ran to crack the atmospheric seals. Within minutes, the two heavily loaded hovercraft slid out of the cargo hatch.

After several weeks aboard ship, each crewman assigned to the various teams found it a distinct pleasure to breathe the fresh and delightfully fragrant air of the virgin world. The planet was so like their home world that several felt brief nostalgia for the world they were not scheduled to see for another solar rotation. But with the entire alien world to chart, explore, and study, nostalgia was a luxury only allowed Planetary Scout crewmen for brief seconds at a time.

It was the second day when Nathan Blackbird came across the pitiful grave. His shrill whistle called his teammates from their tasks, and within a short time his find was the focus of all the various experts that could conceivably be placed aboard a Pioneer Exploratory Service Scout. Here, for the first time in the history of the Empire, traces of an intelligent, if extinct, race had been discovered! The clutched scraps of artificial fabrics, still impervious to the elements, testified to the advanced state of the dead creature's civilization.

Rapidly the archaeologists took over the pit. In record time, the complete skeleton of the giant native of this new planet was excavated. Within hours, through the ingenious use of wires and liberal quantities of glue, the shape of a giant placental mammal took shape under the skilled hands of the Scout biologists and anthropologists.

Only the setting sun brought their frenzied work to a halt. After carefully protecting their unique construction and excavation pit for the night with an impenetrable force-field, the exhausted crewmen loaded up the hovercraft and headed back to their scout ship for a hot meal and the opportunity to catch a little sleep.

As the Captain strode deliberately into the Control

Room, the entire crew stood straight and looked expectantly at their commander. Sensing the tangible anxiety their captain emitted, and knowing a call had just shunted to them through n-space directly from Home World, they waited for the forthcoming announcement. Captain Hawk sighed, and then abruptly broke the pregnant silence.

"Ladies and gentlemen, I regret to inform you that the news from home is grave. The Empire has been torn asunder by violent civil strife. All ships have been urgently recalled, and we have been instructed to return at once to put our ship at the Emperor's disposal. He will need every ship he can put into service to battle the Rebel Alliance.

The rebels have somehow obtained a new super-weapon that releases unbelievable amounts of energy. As you all know, a basic tenet of our science states that the atom, the smallest unit of matter, is not naturally further divisible except in the superheated crucible of a star, or in the case of the breakdown of certain heavy metals, which our scientists do not pretend to understand.

It now seems, however, that our enemies may have discovered the secret of selectively separating the building blocks of the atom itself. Only that would explain the devastating setbacks our armed forces have suffered.

Entire fleets have been blown from the heavens . . . At any rate, our hour of departure is set at 18:30 Home Planet time tomorrow. It goes without saying that the discovery of this planet is a breakthrough of incredible significance. I pray to merciful God that we may have the peace required to make use of what we have discovered here . . . But before we leave this planet, I want to feel that we have made at least a little progress in the conundrum that faces us here. For now, I would like to hear at least a preliminary report."

"Sir', said the Chief Archaeologist, 'there are entire cities to be excavated here. The ruins stretch for square kilometers!"

"Sir', said the Chief Biologist, 'the native race consisted of almost hairless, mammalian creatures that walked on their two hind limbs."

"Captain,' responded the team's physicist and Chief Science Officer. He ruffled his feathers as he spoke, a sure sign of agitation. 'The radiation here is far above natural limits. Thus, it is necessary to postulate that these creatures may have caused their own extinction by some technique of inadvertently or willfully releasing the energy of the atom. The Human Race, as I believe they called themselves, if my deciphering of their hieroglyphics is correct, may have caused mass suicide."

The Captain moved decisively, and spoke in his commanding tone. "Okay, my little ducklings. You are the best crew I ever had. I regularly ask the impossible of you, and you have never yet let me down. Well, I have a big one for you this time. We will lift off on time tomorrow, and I want some serious meat in those reports. I figure you have about three days of work to do, and less than one day to do it in. Get to it, and make me proud. Move it!"

The ship crew slaved through the night, and the ship was fueled and prepared on time. The various anthropological and biological teams worked at their external sites until the last moments, but still managed to board on time. There they found the flight crew ready and perched at their posts. The rest were safe in their protective stasis fields.

Captain Hawk didn't turn in his command seat, but he called out to his faithful crew. "Is everyone strapped down? Fields on? When the little row of lights silently indicated that all members of all departments were accounted for, he continued.

"OK, ducklings, hold tight. Here we go!" With a sense of frustration and foreboding, the captain slapped the master-rocket control. The chemical rockets roared and the ship computer aimed the vessel for the invisible home world some hundred light-years away. Once free of the gravity-well of the planet, he would turn on the Haskell Warp generators, and they would slip into n-space. Through the shortcut of n-space, the journey of a hundred light-years would take no more than ten planet-rotations.

Suddenly the navigator yelled out in surprise. "Captain, we got an unidentified flying object ! It's close, and its got a radar lock on us!"

"Damn it, Nav, give me some data!"

"It looks like a Home Planet ship, sir! It seems to be painted in anti-royalist red, and . . . it's attack radar just went hyper!"

"Shields up! Until we are out of the gravity well, we are just going to have to take whatever it throws at us."

"Shields are up, Captain. They are designed to stop anything short of a battle cruiser, so we - Sir! We got a hot missile coming our way!"

"Relax, Nav. What is the rating of the shields?"

"Approaching 97%, Captain."

"So what are you worried about?"

"Captain,' shouted the Chief Science Officer, 'our capacitors over-loaded! The whole control system just shut down! Whatever they shot at us, it released unbelievable amounts of radiation!"

The Captain looked directly at his Chief Science Officer.

"I wonder if . . .?"

Does hell exist? What is purgatory? Can one man's hell be another man's heaven? Here is one man's adventures. This speculative story was published in the Spring 2004 edition of Gateway, a Christian e-magazine.

14. VALKYRIES

"Close up, Chetowsky!"

"Hey, Sergeant. I just found Wilson's replacement."

"Then get him to his feet. I got a bad feeling. The Hairys are coming real soon!"

"Okay, Newbie. You heard the Sarge. On your feet!"

"Wow. I feel terrible. Where am I?"

"Time enough for that later, kid. Head for the open meadow - just as fast as you can!"

"Okay. Just let me grab my rifle!"

"Say kid, just what kind of shooter is that?"

"It's an M -19. It became standard G.I. issue a couple a months ago."

"That thing work on single fire?"

"Sure. Full-auto. Three shot burst, or single fire."

"Then put it on single fire, and do it now. Something tells me you're going to need it real soon!"

"Uh, Chetowsky, who exactly are we fighting?"

"They're big and hairy, and they stink. Don't worry about it. You'll know when you see them. And Newbie, when the Hairys attack, I want you to fire very sparingly.

One bullet, one man. Got it?"

"It's Okay, Chetowsky. I got extra clips."

"What's your name, Newbie?"

"Parzelli, sir."

"Then listen to me, Parzelli. It's not okay. You're going to need every bullet you have. There's a lot more of them than us. One bullet, one man. That clear? They might shoot a few arrows or throw spears when they come, but that's just the preliminaries.

They're going to take their casualties and then they're going to try and close on us. They use these big bloody swords and axes. They just love to cut us to pieces. We waste ammo, we get shredded. That clear enough for you?"

"Yah. Sorry, Chetowsky."

All of a sudden, the sergeant's voice boomed. "All right, you pansies, form up! Tight circle! Here they come!"

"Hey, Chetowsky. The guy is buck-naked, and he's waving an almighty big sword. Do we shoot him?"

"Newbie, he's a berserker, and you're close man. If you don't shoot him real quick, he's going to slice and dice you!"

The new recruit stood and emptied his clip into the wildly charging man. The sheer power of the slugs first stopped the charge in mid-air, and then sent the man hurtling backwards.

Chetowsky frowned. "Nice shooting, Newbie."

"Thanks Chetowsky."

"Course, you probably just condemned yourself to a very painful death. What's your caliber?"

"5.56"

"Too bad, most of us only have 7.63. Yep, you're going to be sorry tonight."

"So where can I get some more ammo?"

"You can't, Newbie. When you wake up tomorrow,

you'll be re-supplied."

"You mean if I wake up. You just told me I'm not going to make it to tomorrow alive."

"That's not quite what I said, Newbie. I said that you're going to have a very painful death today."

"Then tomorrow really doesn't matter a whole lot to me, does it?"

"More than you know, Newbie."

The sergeant spoke. "All right, pansies! Here come the rest of the bastards!"

"Hey, Chetowsky! These guys look like a bunch of God-damned Viking warriors."

"Good guess, Newbie. Now shoot 'em, one at a time. If you run out of ammunition, fix your bayonet, and good luck to you."

The veteran soldiers stood shoulder to shoulder and calmly fired into the ring of attacking warriors. The circle held, though it was quickly surrounded by the bodies of dozens of fur-clad barbarians. At last there were no new targets, and the new man turned again to Chetowsky.

"Just where the hell am I? Why the hell are we fighting barbarians out of the Dark Ages?"

"Kid, you're going to know more than you want to by the end of the day. Sergeant?"

"Yeah, Chetowsky?"

"Can we call a break and give the Newbie lesson number one?"

"What the hell, why not? It's not like we got anything important to do. OK, you pansies, we'll take five right here. Corporal, I want four scouts out ASAP. On the double! Let's move!"

"Sarge, we did the entire party. We should have a while."

"OK. Two scouts out."

The new man stared around in bewilderment. "What lesson you talking about?"

Chetowsky smiled briefly. "Just stay where you are and watch the dead Hairys, real careful-like."

"I don't see nothing. They're just lying . . . Holy cow! Where did those babes come from?"

"Tell me what you see."

"If I tell you what I see, you're going to think I'm crazy!"

"Try me."

"Beautiful blondes, and they're almost naked! Can we get closer?"

"Don't move your ass off the ground, boy! There's no way you want to mess with those beauties!"

"But they're taking the bodies away."

"And?"

"They just seem to disappear into some kind of rainbow, along with the bodies. Just what the hell are those broads?"

"We don't know, but we got a theory. It's Swede's story, so I'll let him tell you. Swede! Tell the Newbie what he just saw."

"Sure Chetowsky. As far as ve know, boy, them are Valkyries."

"Valkyries? Who, or what, are Valkyries?"

"Before they became Christian, my ancestors worshiped, amongst others, the god Odin. Odin vas supposed to live in a place called Valhalla, 'the Hall of Slain Varriors'. Varriors who die bravely in battle vere brought to his hall by beautiful maidens called Valkyries."

"So what happens to the dead guys there?"

"I don't know for sure, but I know I have killed the same ugly bastard a couple of dozen times. They seem to get made vhole again, and then they come after us again and again."

"Why? For what purpose?"

"I don't know, boy. Legend has it that the heroes of

Valhalla are supposed to party and fight every day, until Ragnarök."

" Ragnarök?"

"Vhat you vould call Doomsday, the day vhen the Viking varriors will march out the 540 doors of Odin's palace to fight against the giants."

"Now let me see if I got this straight. Those 'Hairys' we just wasted will be taken back to some palace where they will be miraculously 'cured'. Then they get to drink and screw all night. Then, come morning, they get their swords and come after us again."

Chetowsky smiled. "Not bad. I think you got it."

"You really expect me to buy that?"

For reply, Chetowsky undid the buttons to his shirt and shrugged it off. The new recruit just stared in fascination at the myriad scars.

"What on earth happened to you?"

"I've been dying off and on for something like thirty years. Every time the big Hairys get me, they cut me to pieces. I die. Next morning, the wounds are healed, and the Hairys are after me again."

"You - You're not bullshitting me, are you?"

"I wish I was, kid."

"Where the hell am I?"

"Newbie, what happened to you just before you woke up here?"

"That's kinda embarrassing."

"Let me take a wild guess. You killed someone."

"Close. I was serving with the U.N. Peacekeeping force in Bosnia. I was manning a checkpoint one evening when this beautiful young broad came along on her bicycle. She was about sixteen and had great tits. She got real scared when I pointed my rifle at her.

I told her I had to do a strip search before she could pass. The silly cow believed me and stripped off her clothes. Well, one thing led to another, and before I knew it, I was jumping her bones."

"And what happened after that?"

"Isn't that enough?"

"Kid, every single one of us here is a murderer. You haven't finished your story yet."

"Well, the next day I was walking in town when I spotted the little cow with two ugly-looking men. She pointed at me, and her two boyfriends came after me. I pulled my sidearm and shot the first guy, but the second one had a big bloody knife out, and he gutted me."

"And the next thing you know is that you woke up here."

"That's about the size of it. What about you?"

Chetowsky sighed. "I was in 'Nam. I had a real prick for an officer. His stupidity got a couple of my buddies killed. One day we caught a little gook with a couple of grenades hidden in a sack of rice. We blew the sucker away, but I stashed one of the grenades.

Two days later we were on Recon, when we were pinned down by enemy fire. Somehow, A VC grenade landed right behind my favorite officer. It splattered parts of him over a fifty foot radius."

"You fragged the bastard!"

"Nobody could prove anything. But the Lord knew what I did. A couple of weeks later I caught an AK-47 slug, and then I woke up here."

"You say everybody here is a murderer?"

"Swede, tell the Newbie your story."

"Sure, Chetowsky. I had just immigrated to New York from Sveden, vhen the South declared var on the Union."

"The Union? Wait a minute, you talking about the American Civil War?"

"Dat's right. Soon after I arrived, I found myself marching vis General Sherman through the Shenandoah Valley. Ve found a couple of Confederate girls hiding in a hay loft. Ve raped them, and vhen they would not stop screaming, ve strangled them. Den ve burned the barn to hide the evidence. A day later I caught a stray ball, and I voke up here."

"But - but that makes you . . ."

"Yep. Over von hunnerd and fifty years old."

"But that can't be."

"Vhy not? Vhen you are dead, you are dead for a long time."

"You're telling me I'm dead?!"

"Ve are all dead, boy."

"Then what are we doing here?"

"Dat is a question I have been asking for a long time."

"Surely somebody knows!"

"There is nobody to ask."

"Then let's get out of here!"

Chetowsky spoke up. "Kid, do you think we haven't tried?"

"What happens?"

"To the east and west, you reach a sheer, unclimbable cliff. To the south, there is a giant pit. We call it the Hellhole."

"How come?"

"When you get tired of marching and fighting, then you can take the Long Dive down the hole. Any one who does that, never comes back."

"So what happens to them?"

"Search me, kid. There's only one way to find out, and I'm not ready to try it yet."

"When you guys first found me, you said that I was a replacement for some guy called Wilson."

"That's right."

"Did he make the Long Dive?"

Chetowsky looked thoughtful for a few moments. "I don't think so. Sometimes one of us just disappears. We don't know how or why."

"So what is north of here?"

"You can see it if you climb one of the trees. It's a massive mountain."

"So why don't we go there?"

"Where do you think the big Hairys live?"

"So what is stopping us from, hypothetically, from moving in and appropriating the palace, the booze, and the broads? We got the guns."

The Swede spoke. "Ve tried it, sonny. No matter how many ve kill, dey just keep on coming, more and more of them. The Valkyries can re-cycle them faster than ve can kill them, until the ammunition runs out. That's vhen ve all die."

"Until the next morning when it all starts again?"

Chetowsky grinned. "Newbie, you learn fast."

"So what's with the 'big Hairys'"?

"This ain't no kind of hell for them, kid. They're doing what they always wanted to do. Hunt, fight, drink, and make love."

One of the scouts arrived, panting. "The Hairy reinforcements have arrived. Get ready!"

Chetowsky stood next to the new kid. "This is not going to be a good day, Newbie."

"What's wrong?"

"After that last attack, we are almost out of ammo. It makes the big Hairys real happy when we run out. They're going to get to close with us today. - Shoot frugal, and shoot accurately, Parzelli!"

Giant blond warriors dressed in furs and metal armor burst from the nearby bushes. They stopped just long enough to hurl their spears, and then advanced, waving their great swords and shouting "Odin! Odin!"

One by one, the rifles sounded an ominous 'click.' Without hesitation, the soldiers slipped their bayonets on the rifles and prepared to fight for their lives. Hearing the clicks, the surviving Vikings formed a shield wall and advanced steadily. The bearded faces behind the shields grinned at the soldiers.

"Oh, shit! Chetowsky, what happens now?!"

"Do your best to defend yourself, kid. Eventually some bastard will get you and you're going to fall. The pain will be bad until sometime after sunset. When you awake in the morning, you'll have some nice new scars, but you'll be fine and ready for action."

"Damn it, Chetowsky! It's like I'm trapped in some kind of damn purgatory!"

"You finally figured it out, kid."

The Vikings closed the distance quickly. The accurate rifle fire threw back the ones in front of Parzelli. One however, made it through the hail of lead. The giant, just out of Chetowsky's peripheral vision, raised his battle axe to cleave the man in two. When his rifle clicked empty, Parzelli cursed and threw himself in front of the charging Viking.

He threw up his empty rifle, but it was too little, too late. The blade of the giant axe bit into the nylon handle, and the weapon was torn from Parzelli's hands. The blade ricocheted into his abdomen, and he felt sudden stabbing pain. He reached for his combat knife, but the axe had cut major arteries. Parzelli felt the last of his strength slipping away.

Parzelli felt a deep contentment. He opened his eyes slowly, to see that he was supported in mid-air by two beautiful women. They were dressed all in white, and had golden wings which were providing lift for all three of them. Strangely, in spite of his normal fear of heights, Parzelli no fear at the ever-increasing elevation. He spoke.

"Are you Valkyries?"

The vision on his right smiled. "They are the servants of Lucifer. We serve a greater power."

"What is happening?"

"Just relax. You have done a very brave thing today. Your Father has asked for you to come and sit on his right hand side."

"But my father died years ago."

The vision smiled. "Then you will meet two fathers today. In the name of Sweet Jesus, we are taking you Home."

Parzelli's eyes shifted downward. Far below, he could see a fresh ring of Vikings overrun his former companions. Most of the riflemen were already slumped on the ground.

His eyes shifted upward again. As Parzelli climbed towards the blinding light, sweet music filled his ears.

This is yet another short story that emanated from my university days. The theme reflects the time, when two world powers fought a hot war around the world through the use of various proxies. James Bond was all the rage, with his licence to kill, and vital secrets were leaked to both sides. This story sat around in a binder for years, until some twenty years later I found it and decided to resurrect it.

15. TO KILL A SPY

Samuel Benson was called into his administrator's office. He had a momentary fear that his dreaded secret had been found out. It was impossible, but what did his boss want? He pushed open the door with great trepidation.

"Sam, I have received official instructions from Washington that you are to attend a top level meeting about Project Torch in Denver, tomorrow morning. All arrangements have been made for your transportation, and my secretary will give you the particulars on your way out. I need not remind you that this is easily the most secret meeting in the country, so watch yourself! Good luck!"

So it was settled. Samuel Benson had been called a thousand miles to attend the all-important final briefing. But most important, he had not been found out. No one knew that he was a traitor to the country of his birth.

As he climbed down from the shiny metallic DC 13, he saw his personal escort waiting patiently for him. Big burly men, each wore a mustache and similar shiny black shoes. He thought, wryly, that with the FBI goons escorting him, he had less freedom than a prisoner at San Quentin. From the government transport jet, he was hustled into a sleek black limo, and he and his police escort roared down the highways to Military Intelligence Headquarters, Western Division.

He walked through the main doors and immediately sensed the electronic sentries. The chemical sensors, sonic scanners and metal detectors all whirred silently and invisibly. Samuel knew that technicians scanned their instruments for signs of unusual odors, body densities or hints of metal or plastic weapons. Guns, knives and even pointed combs were contraband in this, the innermost sanctum of a security conscious nation.

Finally, after his retinas and fingerprints were computer matched, Samuel Hamilton Benson, Colonel of Military Intelligence, was permitted entry into the great secret fort that comprised HQ. As his suitcase was carried off by the efficient guards, he knew it, too, would be painstakingly checked by experts. No one, however, more than glanced at the Eagle-brand pen jutting out of his breast pocket.

Sam took the seat which had his name inscribed on the wooden plaque. Someone's third assistant secretary had ordained that this was to be his seat during the conference, and he was not about to argue.

Even as Sam sat and gazed at his fellow scientists and military and security officials, the General in charge of the briefing introduced the speaker. This man strode boldly into the room and took his seat at the podium. Sam watched the man staring at the greatest minds in America. Before him the mysterious speaker saw the men who had planned the secret invasion of Cuba. He saw the men who had taken the seed of an idea, sadly bruised from the debacle under the Kennedy administration many years before, and had carefully nurtured it into fruition.

The guest of honor continued to stare back at the audience. No one recognized him, for he was masked. Only his two bright Viking-blue eyes stared out with an icy stare from his black silk mask. Even in this inner sanctum, his identity was too important to be known. Even here, within the inner sanctum of a secretive nation, the security gurus had felt there might just conceivably be a leak.

If their years of secrecy failed and the Russians got wind of the daring plan, the U.S. would not be able to present Russia with a fait accompli. Even the EU and the United Nations might get involved, potentially forcing the American withdrawal. The planners only had one chance to get it right, and that time was now! If word got out prematurely, then the U.S. would not only lose enormous prestige, but would be forced to make a humiliating withdrawal.

The Russians had left Cuba, but it didn't do to rub their noses in the fact that were no longer the paramount power they had been. The Europeans loved the beaches, especially since they didn't have to be shared with the great unwashed American public. The United Nations, powered by a one-vote one-country voting system, could always outvote the U.S. and its faithful allies. No, the only hope was a blitzkrieg, followed instantly by a U.S. appointed puppet government. Well, the government-in-exile was sitting in Miami, just waiting for the word. Entire divisions, tested and blooded in Iraq, sat in their barracks just waiting for the call to arms.

For hours, the geniuses, culled from various government departments and various arms of the military forces, debated the amount and necessity of seapower, of air power, of manpower. The political experts discussed the probable reactions of the other nations; friend and foe alike. The psychologists and sociologists discussed the most effective preliminary approach to the civilian population.

In short, the plan was comprehensively checked and rechecked. No significant detail was excluded, except only one, and that detail sat in the chair labeled Colonel Samuel Benson. For colonel Benson was a 'leak'.

Having already informed his Kremlin bosses of the basics of the plan, it would only be a matter of days before he would finally meet his secret contact and be on his way under the Atlantic to Russia and a new life under its flag. He knew that when, the day before the American landings, the Russians confronted president Dicks with the intimate invasion details, his own life would be worth less than nothing.

He had no desire to test the effectiveness of the government security forces. There had been a few grievous errors, but on the whole he knew them to be damned good. Although a civilized nation, when vital policies are at stake, universal decency had little place. He knew no international Red Cross representative would rescue him from a deep cell if he was so much as suspected. Before the security goons finished with him, he knew he would be glad to tell all. He would beg them to listen. It was not a pleasant subject to think about.

Benson fingered the lethal pen. He wondered if he should risk its use. Given to him for use only in grave emergencies, he contemplated committing one last bold stroke against the Americans before he left the decedent land. He decided it was worth the risk! Sometime within the next 24 hours, he would finally get the word to bolt. He had been assured that all eventualities had been planned for. Possibly within hours, he would be on his way home to a hero's reception.

As the President's personal advisor, wearing his ever-present mask, entered the washroom, he saw nothing. He never saw the silent shadow that matched him, pace for pace, fifty feet behind. As he bent over the sink to wash his hands, he didn't hear the door behind open and close. He didn't see Samuel Benson standing there triumphantly.

Sam knew that this man was vital to U.S. military planning. No other genius had ever brought the U.S. such power. The mind behind that mask had bucked world opinion, and in the face of millions, had expanded U.S. control of many foreign governments. Now, he was about to pull off another coup; Cuba.

Sam drew his slim blue pen from his pocket. Taking a firm grip on the end of the ink cartridge, he pulled the cartridge right out of the pen. It slid silently out, until one and half inches were exposed. Remembering his training, Sam aimed the gaping front at the man's side, and turned the eraser at the end until it made a complete rotation within the metal casing. With a hollow 'psst', a slim silver needle leapt from the mouth of the pen, and was hurtled by the compressed carbon dioxide into the unsuspecting victim.

The needle slid easily through the man's shirt and smock, and entered his side. At the slight prick, he turned sideways and gaped at Benson. His mouth, under the mask, was just forming the sound "wh . . . " when the deadly nerve poison took effect. The heart stopped its rhythmic pumping, and the body slid quickly to the floor, where it lay still.

Sam withdrew the needle hastily and, making sure to hold only the very end, flushed the metal sliver down the toilet. Heart attack would be ruled out very quickly if the dart was found in the body! Sam turned to flee the scene, but even as his hand gripped the door, he hesitated. Finally, curiosity overcame him, and he returned to have a furtive glance at that face. Only the President, and perhaps three others, knew who the man was, and Sam was eager to join the select few. He reached down with his gloves and carefully peeled up the black mask.

Samuel Benson perceived a sudden familiarity with the face that stared sightlessly upwards. He could not immediately place it, but he had that face stored somewhere in his memory. Suddenly, with a sinking heart, he realized why it was so familiar. For several months he had studied that face. He had memorized it from all angles, until it was indelibly etched in his memory and he knew it better than his own. He just didn't expect to see it in Security Headquarters. It was the only ticket he had to Russia. He had just killed his contact.

About the Author

After counseling teenagers and adults for over 40 years, Bruce Corbett retired to concentrate on his writing and photography. To date, he has both written and published a collection of Science Fiction short stories, and two Science Fiction novels are coming soon. His biggest project, however, is his series of historical novels based on a fictional hero, Ambrose, set in the time of Alfred the Great.

Other Stories Available From the Author.

In chronological order
HISTORICAL

I. The Ambrose Sagas
1. Ambrose, Prince of Wessex; Trader of Kiev
2. Ambrose, Prince of Wessex; Emissary to Byzantium
3. Ambrose, Prince of Wessex; Southern Journey
4. Ambrose, Prince of Wessex; Journey Home
5. Ambrose, Prince of Wessex; Warrior of the King
6. Ambrose, Prince of Wessex; Gretchen, Future Princess

II. The King Alfred Sagas
1. Alfred the Great; Viking Invasion
2. Alfred the Great; King's Revenge
3. Alfred the Great; Young Edward

III. The King Edward Sagas
1. Alfred the Great; Edward the King
2. Queen Ethelflaed; 'Lady of the Mercians' 2023
3. Elfwynn, Traitor Queen of Mercia   2023

IV. The First English Kings Sagas
1. Athelstan, First King of England   2023
2. Edmund, King of England   2023
3. King Eadred of England   2024

SCIENCE FICTION

Bruce Corbett's Speculative Short Stories
The Goldmines of Alpha Centauri   (coming soon)
The Vuorran Pogrom   (coming soon)

The above novels are available worldwide as e-books from your favorite online book sellers, and the paperbacks are available from Amazon and Drafts2Digital.